Sign up for our newsletter to hear
about new and upcoming releases.

www.ylva-publishing.com

OTHER BOOKS BY A.L. BROOKS

A Heart to Trust
Dare to Love
Never Too Late for Heroes
The Long Shot
Write Your Own Script
One Way or Another
Up on the Roof
Miles Apart
Dark Horse
The Club

A.L. BROOKS

ACKNOWLEDGEMENTS

To the Ylva team—five years ago you published my debut, *The Club*, and here we are with a sequel eleven books later! Thank you for giving my stories a chance.

To Michelle for a fab editing experience; it was great to learn from you!

To my beta readers, Erin, Katja, Mari, and Amy. As ever, you gave me awesome feedback that helped lift the story from its humble beginnings as a "shall I write this or not?" piece to where we are now. Thank you!

And to my partner, Tanja, for always supporting every single word I write.

DEDICATION

To all of you who loved *The Club* and wrote to tell me so—you helped make a debut author's dream come true.

CHAPTER 1

MANDY

Mandy stood in the middle of the Green Room and inhaled deeply. Her heart raced, but she understood why—this view just couldn't get old. Nor could her pride at what she'd achieved here.

But it was almost opening time for the night, and she couldn't stand here wallowing in emotion.

She gazed around her club's main room, running a critical eye over every detail. The room was spotless; minutes earlier she'd inspected every nook and cranny and found nothing awry. Chairs and stools had been positioned in a seemingly random pattern against the walls, but there was still plenty of room for people to stand if they preferred. The centre bar, like every item of furniture, was clean but also sanitized with its stools lined up like regimental soldiers.

She frowned. That seemed almost too perfect. People needed to feel comfortable here if they were going to consider taking their clothes off. She walked over to the bar and rearranged a couple of the tall stools, leaving them at slight angles to each other. Better.

The Blue Room was next and passed her usual inspection with flying colours, as did the Red Room, where the cross was polished to a deep shine and the leather on the spanking benches gleamed in the full lights she currently had switched on. Thank God for the well-paid but extremely discreet cleaning company. Over the past eighteen months or so that the club had been open, she'd never found fault with their work, and their prices were worth it.

She walked back towards the room's bar and over to the control panel to dim the lights to their standard, sultry evening setting, glancing back into the room once she'd done so. *Perfect.*

"Hey." Dee's voice came from behind her.

Mandy turned and smiled at her assistant. "Good evening." But then she frowned at Dee's serious expression. "Everything okay?" The way Dee bit at her lip seemed like something was much more wrong than a malfunctioning bar tap or whatever she might have found in the club that Mandy had somehow missed. *Is she ill? Facing a crisis at home?* Her obvious worry was mystifying.

Dee ran a hand through her short blonde hair. "Um, yeah. Sort of." She puffed out a breath. "So, I need to talk to you."

Mandy's concern spiked. "Just tell me. Are you all right?"

"I am!" Dee placed one hand on Mandy's arm. "But I have some news. I…I've been… Well, I'm just going to come out and say it: I got offered a position on a lesbian cruise ship."

Mandy blinked at her. "A cruise ship?" she echoed dumbly. Did she mean what Mandy thought…?

Dee's gaze suddenly flew to her feet. "Yeah," she said after a long moment. "Entertainment manager. It's a big step up in responsibility, and, of course, there's loads of travel."

She's been with us since we opened; the random thought occurred to her out of nowhere. "This isn't you asking for a vacation, is it?" she said finally, a bit helplessly. A moment ago, everything in her world had been lined up to perfection. She liked the orderly little world she'd created here, and now it was suddenly all being disrupted by one decision made by someone else and completely out of Mandy's control.

"You know I've always wanted to see more of the world..." Dee had managed to look up at Mandy, her expression hopeful.

Well, fuck. Mandy sighed. From somewhere inside her, she summoned up a smile. "It sounds perfect for you." Her stomach twisted at the thought of losing Dee; she'd been with Mandy even before the club's opening night, now that she thought about it, helping her with the final four weeks of setup and finishing touches. Dee had been nearly as invested in the club as Mandy was herself, and the thought of not having her by her side—

"I just don't think I can pass it up." Dee was fidgeting with the hem of her shirt, but at least she kept her view on Mandy now, which was a good sign.

"And you shouldn't." Mandy gave her a quick hug, something they rarely shared, but clearly, the situation warranted it. She didn't want to make Dee feel guilty over this. She had every right to leave, of course, even if it was going to inconvenience Mandy to hell. "I'm very happy for you."

Dee relaxed her shoulders. "I'm not going for another couple of months, don't worry. And I already had a thought about who could take my position."

Mandy quirked an eyebrow.

"Nina," Dee said confidently. "You should promote her. She knows this place like the back of her hand. And she *loves* it here, you know that."

Mandy nodded slowly, musing over the idea. She wouldn't have thought of it herself—Nina was such a high-spirited personality, maybe even a bit distractible—but once she learned a task, she was solid. It definitely had some promise, given Nina was so familiar with the setup, the clientele. Maybe she could do it.

"And, I thought," Dee continued, her words coming out a bit faster, "you could also use the opportunity to maybe recruit another one or two people to help out around here. You know how successful we've been lately, and only having the two of us always running the office stretches us all a bit. Especially you." Dee paused, then plunged on. "I thought you might want some time free at the weekends. To get out a bit. I know you've been pretty lonely since Rebecca died. You haven't dated anyone since, and—"

Mandy held up one hand. "Rebecca and I never dated. We were only ever friends." Well, that was a nugget of information she'd never meant to share with Dee.

Dee's mouth fell open. "You and she weren't a couple? But I thought...I thought you were in love with her?" She frowned in confusion.

Mandy threw her a rueful smile. "Those statements are not mutually exclusive." She shook her head; might as well explain it all now—Dee was leaving in a couple of months, what did secrecy matter anymore? "She was my best friend, but she was straight, and I committed the cardinal lesbian sin of falling in love with her."

"Oh, Mandy, no way! Did you even get a chance to tell her?"

"She knew." Now it was Mandy's turn to look away uncomfortably. "She knew, and she never said a word about it—until she was dying." She couldn't help it: her voice cracked.

"Fuck, Mandy, I had no idea." Dee hooked her thumbs in her jeans pockets. "Sorry."

Mandy waved off her apology. "And as for me hiring extra staff so that I can date again, well, I haven't dated anyone in years. And I can't imagine I'm going to start now." She chuckled hoarsely. "I think that boat has sailed. I'm too set in my ways to go through all of that nonsense of getting to know someone."

Her chest tightened a tad as the vision of being on her own for the rest of her days flashed before her; it suddenly didn't seem so appealing. *Odd.* "But I do like your idea of talking to Nina about taking over. Thank you for suggesting it."

Dee nodded, exhaling deeply again, but this time it seemed more from relief than from dread.

Mandy took advantage of the moment and clapped her hands together. "Now, we need to get on with our night's work," she said. "Thank you for the heads-up and for giving me such a good amount of notice. I will miss you, very much, but I am very excited for what this opportunity can give you, so grab it with both hands and don't let go, okay?"

Dee's eyes glistened. "I will. And… Well, please, just think about the extra staff idea, will you?" She grinned. "*And* the dating. There's a lot left in you to give someone, you know. You're not *that* old."

The cheeky little… Mandy made to slap her butt, and Dee deftly skipped out of the way.

"Downstairs. Now!" Mandy pointed at the door to the hallway, struggling to contain her own laughter.

"Yes, ma'am!" Dee winked and strode off.

And just like that, things were back to normal between them. Really, she reflected, it could be worse. Dee had given her lots of time to get used to the idea of her not being around. And Nina would learn quickly, especially with Dee training her. That thought alone gave her comfort.

By the time they opened the club at nine on the dot, Mandy was back on track, which was a good thing because two women were already waiting to gain entry. From then on, it was the usual slow but steady build-up toward ten, when most women started to appear.

She had just returned from her first business-hours tour of the rooms a little after ten when the door buzzer sounded behind her, prompting her to swivel in the office doorway and step out into the dimly lit hall. As always, readying to greet a new visitor, she got a buzz at what she'd created here at the club and the number of women who wanted to use it. She'd definitely created something her younger self would have loved. A rueful smile twisted her lips as she walked to the door—it was a shame her older self was rather past all this. Not only was Mandy not about to start dating, she was not about to go looking for fleeting pleasures—not at her own club nor anyone else's.

Of course, she took a moment to proudly note, no one else's club in the UK was like hers—created specifically for women looking to satisfy their needs in a safe, consensual space where no one would ever, ever judge them.

She slid back the small shutter that covered an opening in the door at eye-height. The simple security measure ensured that no visitors could enter unless she wanted them to. The club wasn't widely advertised, and she'd been careful to make it clear it was only for women, cis or trans, and non-binary identifying lovers of women only, but it paid to be cautious. Her worst nightmare had always been a group of aggressive drunken men trying to gain entry. Thankfully, that had never happened.

"Hi," the woman on the other side of the door said, her voice timid. "Am I in the right place?"

Mandy took a couple of seconds to assess her, experience counting for everything each time she did this. "Yes, you are. Come on in."

She stepped back, pulled back the security bar and opened the door.

The woman walked into the hallway. She was probably late forties, about five or six years younger than Mandy's fifty-five, with nondescript light brown hair that held a little natural curl, and she was dressed in a plain blue shirt over jeans.

Mandy shut the door behind her and turned to face her. "Welcome to the club. My name's Mandy, and I'm the owner."

"H-hello. I'm-I'm Lindsey."

Nervous as hell. "Hi, Lindsey. It's nice to meet you. You're new here, right?"

The woman nodded, her eyes wide as she cast glances all around her. Her gaze landed on Dee in the office, and she blinked a couple of times.

"My assistant, Dee." Mandy was pleased when Dee looked up at the sound of her name, and, as always, waved in a casual, friendly manner. Mandy had trained all her staff to be welcoming and easy-going with every customer, but it was still lovely to see it in action.

Lindsey lifted a shaking hand in response.

Oh, wow, she's beyond nervous. Hm, is she really ready for this? "So, shall I tell you how this all works?"

Lindsey looked back at her and licked her lips. "Yes, please."

"We are classified as a private club, for which you will pay a membership fee to use the facilities on offer. This membership is for one evening only and costs twenty pounds." She waited until Lindsey nodded her understanding before continuing. "There are three rooms, identified by the colour of the light above their doors—green, blue, and red. The Green Room is the one you will enter first; the others lead off from that so you can't stumble into them by accident. Okay so far?"

"Yes. Okay." Lindsey's posture eased a tad.

"The Green Room is what we call the vanilla room, but by that we simply mean no strap-ons and no BDSM. Strap-ons can be used in Blue, and BDSM is restricted to the Red Room."

Lindsey's eyes widened at *strap-on* and *BDSM*, and Mandy would have bet her house Lindsey would only be visiting Green tonight.

"In each room, there's a bar with a full range of non-alcoholic and alcoholic drinks. Our bartenders are also there to act as, shall we say, security—if anything happens that you are not comfortable with, or they see something happening that is outside the rules, they will step in. Sitting at the bar, or at the centre table in each room, is a safe zone. You cannot touch or initiate contact with anyone there."

Lindsey nodded. "Good to know."

Mandy smiled. "Everyone new says that, and, trust me, everyone respects it, so please do let me know if anyone suddenly doesn't. Now, if you are interested in contact with someone, you can either approach them or wait for them to approach you. Anyone standing along one of the walls is giving their consent to be approached, however they are *not* giving consent for sexual contact until that's been negotiated and agreed between the parties. Understood?"

Her visitor relaxed her shoulders. "Yes. That's all really clear, thanks." Her voice was a little stronger now.

Good. "Any other questions?"

Lindsey flushed and looked at her feet. "Do I—do I *have* to do anything?"

"Absolutely not," Mandy said gently and waited until Lindsey met her eye once more before continuing. "If you just want to watch, even for just ten minutes and then leave, you go right ahead." She paused, then offered a final piece of advice that she reserved only for these most nervous of newbies. "But remember, this is one place where you can find very like-minded souls and be free to try out something new without any fear of recrimination or embarrassment. Everyone here wants exactly the same thing, in essence—the freedom to be as sexual as they like on their own terms."

Lindsey's wide smile at that moment lit up Mandy's whole week.

The door buzzed again before she could say anything else. "One moment, let me just get that." Even though Dee could get the door this time, she thought the pause would do Lindsey good, give her some thinking time. "Why don't you wait a little over there and I'll be right back?"

Lindsey nodded enthusiastically and stepped to the side.

Mandy waved Dee away as she approached the door. "No worries, I've got this."

She opened the shutter and saw a handsome woman about her own age on the step. The woman seemed startled to see

Mandy peering back at her through the gap in the door and Mandy bit back a smile. "Hi, do you know where you are?"

The woman stared for a moment, then seemed to remember she needed to speak. "Yes, uh, yes I do."

"Good." Mandy opened the door and let the woman in. "I'll be with you in just one moment, okay?"

"Sure." The woman stepped into the hallway, her gaze pinned on Mandy.

Why is she staring at me like that?

Granted, many of the women who walked through the door to the club would stare at Mandy, their nerves plain to see in the way their gazes seemed to beseech Mandy to put them at ease—not unlike Lindsey over there in the corner. But there was something different about the way this woman looked at her, her green-eyed gaze holding Mandy's. She felt the urge to ask, "Do I know you?" but that was ridiculous. She didn't do much socialising outside the club, not even with her fellow neighbourhood business owners. After all, the point of the club was its discretion.

"Right, um, one moment." Mandy stepped back, flustered but not sure why.

She turned to Lindsey. "So, how are you doing? Think you'll stay with us a little while?"

Lindsey's blush this time was softer, not quite covering her whole face. "Yes, I'd like to." She handed over a twenty and smiled shyly. "Thank you so much for explaining everything."

"You're welcome. And remember, sitting at the bar or centre table is your safe zone, okay?"

"Got it."

"Excellent." Mandy pointed at the green light above the door at the end of the hallway. "The Green Room is that way. Enjoy your evening."

Lindsey managed a small smile, took a visible breath, then turned towards the door.

Mandy smiled to herself, then turned back to her other visitor, startled to see those green eyes boring into her own once more. *What is it with this woman?* For a moment she wondered if she should call Dee over, whose height and broad shoulders intimidated most people.

But then the woman gave a soft smile, one that nonetheless lit up her whole face. The creases around her eyes widened, and her entire demeanour somehow projected nothing but warmth and gentleness.

Something stirred inside her as she gazed into those eyes, something she thought was long dead and buried. Attraction.

Blimey.

A gentle shiver skittered down her spine as they blinked at each other for a moment.

"You don't remember me, do you?" the blonde asked eventually, her voice as soft as her smile—and holding a hint of self-deprecation.

Mandy wracked her brain, flashing through the clientele she'd seen pass through the club's door in the last year or so, then back further to her times working in other, less specialised clubs. "No, I'm sorry, I don't. Where did we—?"

"Brixton. Maybe twenty-five years ago. At a dance club." The woman grinned sheepishly. "That skanky woman got mad at us for, you know, getting it on in the toilet, and smacked you one. The last time I saw you, you were sat on a bench down the street, trying to fix your bleeding cut lip and—"

Mandy's breath caught. Her mind whirled as her past caught up with her present.

CHAPTER 2

LINDSEY

As she walked through the door from the main entranceway, leaving Mandy's steadying presence behind, Lindsey willed her heart to stop trying to beat its way out of her chest.

Come on, you've been planning this all week. You can't back out now.

Of course, planning something and then carrying it out was sometimes easier said than done.

Still, she *was* here, and she *was* about to walk into a room where women were openly having sex with each other, just as she'd planned. *Oh my God.*

The lighting in the short hallway that led to the room was dimmer than in the main entranceway, but that was understandable. The professional in her admired the setup, and she nodded in approval at the tones Mandy had chosen, the frosted glass globes unobtrusive and ensuring that the light was soft and gentle. She nearly snorted with laughter at the notion of the hallway lit up by fluorescent lights, highlighting absolutely everything. Talk about mood killer. She vaguely wondered if the lighting company she worked for had supplied any of the gear. Wouldn't that be a hilarious coincidence?

She turned a corner, and suddenly the room was in front of her. Her steps faltered as she took a moment to allow her eyes and ears to assess what faced her. A low hum of sultry music played in the background. Over that came the sounds of passion from every corner. The same dim lighting, used in spots along the walls, gave her glimpses of clothed, semi-clothed and, *oh holy shit*, naked women at various points around the room.

Her breathing quickened in pace, and she clenched one hand into a fist and out again to try to release some of her body's tension.

The bar. Get to the bar.

Her legs moved, jerkily at first, and finally she was on a stool at the bar, her shaky legs no longer needing to support her weight.

"Hey," the bartender, a cute, young blonde with a winning dimpled smile, greeted her. "What can I get you?"

"A sparkling water, please." Maybe alcohol later, but now Lindsey wanted her wits about her while she figured out how long she would stay. Even five minutes seemed as if it would be too much, but she also knew, deep down, that leaving so quickly would be a waste of the opportunity. God knew she'd been thinking about this for long enough. Twenty-seven years, to be precise.

"Here you go." The bartender placed the drink on the bar. "Feel free to stay here or move to the centre table with that, if you like. Or, if you head to the wall, you'll find alcoves at shoulder height for drinks and other things."

"Oh. Okay, good to know, thanks." Yeah, like she'd be heading to the wall any time soon.

But maybe the centre table would be a nice idea? Or would that be too pervy, sitting there, watching what everyone else was up to?

She swallowed hard before leaning in to ask quietly, "Is it okay to watch like that?"

The blonde gave her a gentle smile. "Absolutely. It's not considered rude or disgusting. Quite the opposite actually. A lot of customers like to watch to get in the mood before they initiate anything. A lot of customers like to *be* watched to heighten their pleasure. And those who don't, well they generally head for the corners, where it's darkest, for an element of privacy. We have some regulars who come in and all they do is watch, for whatever reason. Nobody minds."

Lindsey absorbed the information, nodding slowly. "Okay, that helps. Thanks."

"You're welcome. By the way, I'm Cassie, and you can ask me anything, okay? I've worked here for a year now, in all rooms, and there's not a lot I don't know about what people want when they come here. And I also know how nervy it can be when you're here for the first time. You should have seen me on my first shift." She dropped her tone to a conspiratorial low. "I honestly didn't know where to look. I think my eyeballs ached for about a week afterwards."

Lindsey laughed, and her shoulders relaxed. She took a sip of her water. "Is it obvious how new I am?"

"Yeah, but that's okay. We all start somewhere."

"Even at my age?"

"Trust me, you're not the oldest newbie I've seen here. At all."

Relief washed through her. "You know, I was told about this place by someone who used to work here. A woman called Jennifer?"

"Oh! Yeah, she's who I took over from. She had to leave because the shift times didn't fit with looking after her kid."

"Yes, that's what she told me. She pulls pints at my local gay bar now, and we got talking one night." Lindsey pulled at the cuffs of her shirt. "I'm newly out as lesbian. I was married to a man for years, but it was, well, pretty awful. And now that I'm out, I don't actually have a clue how to really connect with a woman. I go to the bars and pubs, but the women are all so much younger than me."

Cassie nodded. "The club scene is definitely young. Even I feel a bit out of place sometimes on the rare occasion I head out to one with my girlfriend."

"I did meet one woman more my age one night, but she was super experienced, and I just felt like an idiot around her. Then Jennifer told me about this place. Suggested it might help me get some confidence, or at least knowledge, before I tried actually dating someone."

"Not a bad theory."

"Yeah, I thought so. But it's still pretty daunting being here and thinking about starting something." Lindsey glanced down at herself. "I'm not exactly a supermodel."

"No one here cares about that." Cassie gave her a gentle smile. "They care about who they have sex with. The women who come here, well, most of them just appreciate woman of all ages, shapes, and sizes. They just love women, full stop. Honestly, I've never seen anyone stand against the wall and not hook up." She tilted her head. "But, I mean, let's be honest about that, though: ninety-nine percent of what happens in here is only hook-ups. You're not going to meet the love of your life here."

"Oh, yes! Don't worry, I didn't come in here with that expectation." To be fair, she didn't imagine she'd ever be lucky enough to fall in love with a woman, but she was trying not to be too pessimistic.

"Good." Cassie glanced around as a couple of women approached the bar. "Look, I need to serve them. But can I suggest you head to the centre table? And maybe sit next to that woman with the long auburn hair?"

Lindsey peered over to the table. "Um, why?"

"Let's just say she's a good person to talk to." Cassie gave her an enigmatic smile. "Say hi. See what happens." She tapped the bar with the flat of her hand, held Lindsey's gaze for a moment, then walked down the bar to her new customers.

After another mouthful of her drink, Lindsey turned once more to look towards the centre of the room. The woman Cassie had mentioned sat on the end stool at the table, sipping occasionally from a glass of white wine. She was curvy with deliciously wide hips encased in tight jeans, and she had on a cream, or maybe white, top made of some silky-looking material that swished as she moved.

Should I? Somehow, she didn't think Cassie would have made her suggestion if she didn't think it would be okay. *All right, so let's try it.*

Taking one more fortifying deep breath, she stood and walked over to the empty stool next to the redhead. "Is this seat taken?" Her voice wobbled, of course, but she couldn't help that.

The woman turned to her, and Lindsey realised with a flush of pleasure that the woman was definitely in her age bracket, possibly even a few years older.

Is that why Cassie suggested I talk to her?

The woman smiled. "It is now." Her voice was husky, in a way that sent very pleasurable shivers down Lindsey's spine. *Oh my.* "Please." The woman gestured to the stool.

Lindsey pulled it out and sat, once again grateful that her trembling legs didn't need to hold her up. The woman next to her exuded the kind of earthy sexiness Lindsey had only ever read about in trashy novels. She'd never known it really existed until now.

"I'm Vivian. You're new here, aren't you?"

Am I wearing a badge? "Yes, I am. Lindsey. Nice to meet you."

Vivian looked her up and down and smiled in a way that made Lindsey's breath catch in her throat. "Likewise." She took a sip of her wine. "I'm *not* new here." She winked at Lindsey.

Vivian's flirty sexiness was incredibly easy to respond to, much to her surprise. She smiled. "So you recommend it?"

"Oh, yes." She smiled again. "I have to say, it's delightful to be talking to someone more my own age for once."

"Same." Lindsey chuckled. "All the women I meet in the clubs and bars are so young!"

The throaty chuckle did all sorts of nice things to Lindsey's insides. "Hell, yes. Give me an older, more experienced woman any time."

Cheeks heating with her embarrassment, Lindsey froze. There it was: the conclusion that because she was older, she must be more experienced than she was. *Damn.*

Vivian blinked, then shook her head. "Forgive me, that was a crass assumption. I should have known better."

"That obvious?"

"I am very good at reading body language once I get my head out of my arse."

Lindsey leaned in a little. "You're forgiven." God, this woman was so easy to talk to!

"Good. Now, tell me, what are you here for? I do have a lot of experience, so I'm very willing to help you if you have questions."

"Are you always so forthright?" Lindsey kept her tone light, even though Vivian's directness was rather unsettling.

Vivian waved her free hand. "Oh God, yes. Life is far too short to beat around the bush."

Well, that was one way of looking at it. Hell, why not tell her? It's not like they ever had to meet again after this interaction. "Well, um, I'm very newly out as lesbian. Was married to a man for years. I've, er, never been with a woman, never even kissed one." Her hands twitched at the admissions. "Just spent a *lot* of time fantasising. So I'm here to see if I can fix that so I can gain some confidence in actually trying to meet someone and talking to them and being physical with them and... Well, I suppose I thought doing this might help."

Was this club really the answer?

"I see. Well, you definitely came to the right place for that." Vivian finished her wine, her gaze locked on Lindsey's as she drained the glass.

Lindsey sat stock still, hypnotised by the strength in Vivian's chocolate-brown eyes.

"Mandy explained the rules, yes?" She placed her empty glass on the table. "That someone advertises their interest by finding a point along the wall?"

Her attention drawn to the fullness of Vivian's mouth as it moved, the way her lips glistened in the low light, Lindsey nodded.

"Good." And with that, Vivian slipped off her stool and headed for a space on the wall directly to the left of where she had been sitting.

Fuck. What did I do wrong? Why did she walk aw—?

Vivian looked back over her shoulder as she reached the wall and crooked a finger, beckoning.

Lindsey blinked.

Oh.

Hoping her legs wouldn't betray her, she hurried off her stool, her heart thudding.

When she reached the wall, she swallowed hard before speaking. "Is this… Did you really mean for me to come over?"

"That's exactly what I meant." Vivian winked at her again, then leaned back against the wall. "Are you happy to be over here or…?"

Her mouth was too dry to speak. Somewhere a part of Lindsey's brain wanted to thank Vivian for taking the initiative, for taking away her need to think—or panic.

"Excellent." Vivian's voice had become a purr. "Now, I'll be honest; I'm normally one for getting down to it good and quick, but for you, I'd like to make an exception. I think a little slower would suit you better, hm?"

Oh my God. Lindsey's heart thumped. "Y-yes. Please."

"And I'm also a woman who likes to give the orders. Something tells me that also might suit you—some instruction, perhaps, just to get you started?" She ran one gentle fingertip over Lindsey's cheek and across her lips.

"Yes." Lindsey sucked in a breath as molten desire flooded her body with that one touch. "Instruction. Perfect."

Vivian leaned closer; a hint of her musky perfume teased Lindsey. "I'm also prepared to make another exception for you, just because that mouth of yours looks so ridiculously tempting. I don't usually do such things here, but, Lindsey, would you like to kiss me?"

Wetness coated her. Even the thought of it made Lindsey's cunt clench tightly. "Yes." The word came out as a whisper—all she could manage.

Vivian grabbed the bottom of Lindsey's shirt and tugged her closer. "Slow, remember? Only as far as you're comfortable. Take your time. I know I'm going to enjoy that." She winked again, then placed one hand on the back of Lindsey's neck and pulled her head closer, near enough for Lindsey to smell the hint of wine on Vivian's warm breath as it ghosted over Lindsey's lips.

She shivered, then carefully placed her hands on Vivian's hips. Heat radiated from her ample chest, her stomach, her thighs, all parts of her body which were almost, but not quite, touching Lindsey's. The proximity was dizzying, but even more so was the voluptuousness of Vivian's lips, scant millimetres away from her own.

At Vivian's quick tug on her shirt, Lindsey stopped thinking about those lips and did something about them instead.

The kiss was probably the softest, sexiest thing she had ever experienced. Vivian's mouth was hot on hers, and when her tongue gently licked at Lindsey's bottom lip, she couldn't have stopped opening her mouth if she'd tried.

Vivian's tongue met hers—slowly, languidly—and Lindsey groaned, a sound she felt all the way down to her boots. So this was what kissing was supposed to feel like. Holy mother of God. Everything about it was soft and yet full of passion. It was tender but strong. Everything she'd dreamed of, fantasised about, but never known before.

Those arms wrapped around her waist and finally, thank God, pressed their bodies together. Lindsey was almost overwhelmed with the sensation of Vivian's curves pressed against her own. Vivian's tongue plundering her mouth, diving deep, then out again, then back for more, sent her knees shaking. She was wet, Jesus, so wet! And suddenly her hands had to move, had to touch, had to—

Vivian moaned. Lindsey realised she was cupping the woman's breasts; they were heavy in her hands, so deliciously heavy. The nipples were hard through the softness of the shirt's fabric, pressing into her palms, and she had to pull back from the kiss to look down, to actually see her hands holding a woman's breasts for the first time.

"Wonderful, isn't it?" Vivian's voice was quiet, filled with understanding.

"Yes." Lindsey looked up, wonder coursing through her. "Is this okay?"

"Oh, yes, sweetheart. *Very* okay. Squeeze them. You can be a little rough; I like that."

Lindsey closed her eyes for a moment as yet more heat flashed through her, then did as she was told, kneading the soft mounds between her fingers, pushing into Vivian as she did so. Vivian's breasts were much more than a handful, and all that weight was incredible to play with.

"Fuck, yes, that's it." Vivian threw her head back and pressed herself more into Lindsey's touch. "You can undo my blouse and bra, if you like. Really feel them."

"God, yes, please." It was all still Vivian commanding and her following, but she was okay with that. God knew there was lots she probably wanted to try, but she had no idea how to verbalise any of it right now. Besides, Vivian telling her what to do to her was such a turn-on.

She shifted position, her cunt throbbing as she carefully undid all the buttons down the front of Vivian's silky blouse. A lacy bra peeked out when she parted the two halves of the shirt, and she couldn't resist pinching at the nipples through the fabric, loving the contrast between their hardness and the soft lace.

Vivian sucked in a breath through her teeth. "Yes, perfect. Harder!"

Lindsey took each nipple between her forefingers and thumbs and squeezed, increasing the pressure the more Vivian moaned and writhed. As someone who loved breast play herself, she could well imagine what this was doing to Vivian. Her thighs squeezed together at the thought of Vivian returning the attention on her own breasts.

She momentarily let go so that she could unsnap the bra. It took a couple of goes, and she flushed a little at not getting it the first time, but Vivian's soft kisses on her neck, and her whispered, "Don't worry, I can't even get myself out of my bra sometimes," eased her discomfort.

At the third try, the bra opened, and she swept her hands back around Vivian's ribcage to her breasts, slowly moving over the warm flesh, her heart racing as she cupped them in all their naked glory.

"Jesus, that feels so good," she whispered against Vivian's mouth.

Vivian moaned and kissed her deeply, thrusting her tongue hard into Lindsey's mouth as if she wished to devour her.

Lindsey would be happy to let her.

They stayed like that for who knew how long, kissing intensely, all the while Lindsey stroking, squeezing, and caressing Vivian's abundant breasts.

"God, Lindsey," Vivian finally said in between the hot kisses, "I know I said slow, but you've got me *so* wet and aching. Do you want to touch my pussy? I'd love it if you did, but if not, I can easily take care of things myself."

While the thought of watching Vivian touch herself almost fried Lindsey's brain, she knew she was very ready to do the touching. Desperate to do it, in fact.

"I want to," she said, her voice a rasp she didn't recognise. "So much."

"I am so glad." Vivian gave that throaty chuckle once more. "Undo my jeans and get your hand inside. Now, please."

Lindsey didn't understand how she was still standing, she was so turned on. She could barely move, her cunt aching for something, anything, and as much as she wanted to touch Vivian, she wanted *her* touch too. "Can we—can we touch each other? At the same time?"

Vivian's feral expression made Lindsey's heart skip a beat. "Fuck, yes."

They eased back from each other and simultaneously reached for the buttons on their own jeans. In tandem, they unbuttoned, unzipped, and eased their jeans open.

Lindsey was aware of the roundness of her own belly, until now somewhat disguised by the jeans, but looking down, she saw Vivian's equally soft belly hanging over the top of her lacy underwear and relaxed. She didn't have to pretend. This woman, built the same way as her, wanted Lindsey just the way she was.

"Let me show you what your touches have done to me." Vivian took Lindsey's hand and pulled it to her stomach, easing it inside her underwear. "Just so you know what power you have, no matter how little experience you've had up until now."

She pushed Lindsey's hand down firmly over her crisp hairs and into the soaking wet folds beneath.

Lindsey feared her heart might stop. "Oh my God, that's…" Tears pricked at her eyes. Twenty-seven years waiting, but, by God, it had been worth it for this moment right now. "You feel amazing."

She let herself explore, and the more she did so, sliding her fingers over labia and through copious wetness, the less Vivian held her hand until Lindsey was flying solo, running her fingers over the slipperiness of Vivian's cunt. She'd touched her own pussy, many times over the years, but touching Vivian was familiar and yet so very new all at the same time. She closed her eyes and concentrated on what her fingers could feel: the heat, the wetness, the incredible textures beneath them.

And then, as if her pleasure wasn't enough at the sensation of touching Vivian so intimately, Vivian eased her own hand into Lindsey's cotton underwear and hissed when she encountered the wetness that had pooled there. "All this for me?" she purred, gazing into Lindsey's eyes. "You're spoiling me."

Lindsey grinned, her entire being suddenly infused with such joy that tears threatened once more. "Thank you," she said softly. "For this. For initiating it and—"

But after another of Vivian's deep kisses, Lindsey no longer needed words, just a hungry mouth on hers and strong fingers easing their way along her cunt to her entrance as she did the same to Vivian.

"Yes?" Vivian raised an eyebrow.

"Oh, yes." Lindsey parted her legs. She was so ready to be fucked by this woman.

Vivian nodded. "Me too. Two fingers, hard as you like."

With a groan, she pushed inside Vivian, just as instructed, and Vivian's one finger pushed inside her simultaneously. Their loud, long joint moans hung in the air.

Lindsey dropped her head to lean on Vivian's forehead, her breathing heavy as every push of Vivian's fingers inside her unravelled her that little bit more.

Vivian's breathing was just as loud, her hips canting up to meet each of Lindsey's thrusts. Her choppy breaths were interspersed with "Fuck!" repeated over and over. "More," she said on a grunt. "Three! Now!"

Lindsey obliged, astonished at the heat inside of Vivian, at how tightly she clenched around Lindsey's fingers, at how utterly right it felt to be inside a woman at last. Whatever Vivian was doing to her, she felt filled enough with just one finger, and although she wasn't likely to come from that alone, the fact that Vivian's palm was now flat against her clit and rubbing it so deliciously meant she'd probably reach orgasm soon.

She angled her own hand as much as she could to mirror the position, hoping that it would please Vivian, and bit her lip as Vivian's other hand gripped her waist so tightly, she knew she'd have bruises in the morning. But who the hell cared?

"Yes, yes, yes!" Vivian gasped. "Do that. Faster. Faster!"

Lindsay pumped in and out of Vivian, keeping her palm pressed as tight as she could to the hard clit beneath it. The idea that this sexy woman was riding her hand in wanton pleasure was mind-blowing but oh-so-satisfying. Lindsey had no idea if what she herself was doing was what got Vivian off or if it was more that Vivian could use her, grinding against her to get the purchase she needed. It didn't matter. Not having to particularly worry about technique or finesse meant the fears she'd brought with her to the club tonight stayed locked out of the way.

She lifted her head, watched Vivian as her pleasure played out over her face. She had her eyes shut tight, her mouth slightly open, and even in the dim light, Lindsey could see the flush on her cheeks and neck. "Beautiful," she whispered. "Fuck, you're beautiful like this."

With another moan, Vivian ground down on Lindsey's hand even harder, then came with a keening sound that almost tipped her over the edge herself.

"Fuck, fuck, fuck," Vivian chanted, head tilted back against the wall; her own hand had stilled inside Lindsey.

She didn't mind. Watching Vivian come was thrilling enough, and she drank in the sight, knowing she would never, ever forget this experience, no matter what else happened in her new life.

"Oh, honey," Vivian said after a minute or two, slowly opening her eyes and smiling lasciviously. "You fucked me good."

Pride rippled through her, and Lindsey carefully withdrew her fingers from their hot, swollen encasement. "I'm glad to hear it."

Vivian leaned forward and kissed a sensual line up Lindsey's neck to her ear, then twitched her fingers inside her, making

Lindsey gasp. "But now," she whispered, "we mustn't forget about you, must we?"

Oh, Jesus. That voice. That sound of intent.

"N-no. Please."

Vivian smiled. "Mm, I'll take care of you." She removed her finger from inside Lindsey and slowly stroked up and over her labia to her clit, where she made small, slow circles that tortured Lindsey into breathlessness.

"Oh God, so good." Lindsey didn't recognise her own voice, the strangled, half-moan of a sound it made.

"Uh-huh." Vivian looked down between them at her hand stroking back and forth between Lindsey's legs. "Tell me, sweetheart, do you like to be licked?"

Lindsey froze and stared at her. "I—it's—"

"Hey, it's okay if not," Vivian said softly, "I just thought I'd offer and—"

"I don't know," Lindsey blurted out. "I mean, I don't know if I like it because no one's ever done it to me."

Vivian stilled her hand and blinked a couple of times. "No one?"

Sighing, Lindsey shook her head. "My husband thought it was disgusting."

"What a fool." Vivian's voice dripped with scorn. Then she leaned in and kissed Lindsey softly. "Want to find out what you've been missing?"

There was that seductive purr again, and then Vivian's tongue was licking delicately at Lindsey's ear lobe, then the shell of her ear. Suddenly all Lindsey could imagine was that tongue working elsewhere, and heat shot through her in such a rush, she was light-headed. She nodded, not trusting her voice.

Vivian kissed her, languid but deep, then took a step back. "I suggest we swap positions so you can lean against the wall."

Her mind was still trying to process just what was about to happen to her, but she obeyed.

Vivian took hold of Lindsey's jeans where they were bunched around her hips. "And let's push these down a little too." With a sharp tug, they fell to Lindsey's knees along with her underwear.

She glanced around quickly, feeling exposed. She'd never been so publicly intimate, and she wasn't sure how she felt about it.

"Are we in a dark enough spot for you? We can move to the corner if you wish."

There was only one person Lindsey could see, seated at the table in the centre of the room, but she couldn't see the woman's features at all. *Okay, so if I can't see her clearly, she can't see me.* "No, this is fine." At Vivian's raised eyebrow, she squeezed her waist. "Really. It's good. You can, you know, start."

The grin she got in return was so dirty, it made shivers trickle down Lindsey's spine and all across the back of her thighs. "Yes, ma'am," Vivian said and sank to her knees.

Lindsey dropped her gaze to the woman between her legs, her face so close to Lindsey that she could feel her hot breath skating over her wet pussy. *Oh. My. God.*

Vivian leaned in a little and planted a gentle kiss on Lindsey's mound, just above her clit. "Remember to breathe, honey," she said but didn't wait for any response before moving in just a little farther.

The first touch of Vivian's tongue on Lindsey's labia was probably the most exquisite sensation she'd ever experienced. She couldn't find any word to describe it other than *unbelievable*, and then, as Vivian began to lick more firmly and more rapidly over all of Lindsey's pussy, she gave up on thinking altogether and simply dropped her head back against the wall, eyes closed, her entire body trembling.

Now there were hands cupped on Lindsey's ass, and Vivian pulled her forwards a tad, bringing her pussy closer to her exploring tongue.

Lindsey bent her knees a little—*God, this is going to hurt in the morning but who the fuck cares?*—and opened her legs a little more, as much as her jeans around her knees would allow.

Vivian groaned and dipped her tongue deeper, running it through the creases and folds between Lindsey's labia, lapping softly at her entrance, then swooping back up and, for the first time, running it over her clit. It made Lindsey's hips jerk, and Vivian's chuckle against her wet clit vibrated throughout her body.

"Do you like that?" Vivian asked, gazing up at Lindsey.

The sight of Vivian's lips and chin glistening wet in the dim glow of the room was almost as arousing as what her tongue had just been doing.

Lindsey nodded frantically. "Please don't stop."

"Oh, sweetheart, I'm not stopping until you tell me to." Vivian dipped her head once more.

This time when she licked Lindsey, it was with firmness and more purpose. Now she set a rhythm, a constant, steady one that made pulses of heavy need throb through Lindsey's entire cunt, generating more slick juices that Vivian lapped up with a satisfied moan.

Bracing her hands against the wall, Lindsey surrendered to the pleasure that coursed through her. She'd never known it could be like this, as if her entire body was melting yet turning rigid at the same time. She ached with it, but in the best of ways. Her breathing hitched repeatedly as each turn and twist of Vivian's tongue found new spots that aroused her, new little places that caused her to tremble even more.

She gasped as Vivian slipped one finger inside her. "Oh, *fuuuuuuck*." It was almost too much, the sensations firing off pulses in every nerve of her body.

And then Vivian made some kind of twist with her hand that changed the angle inside her, simultaneously pressing down firmly on Lindsey's clit with her tongue, licking faster and harder.

Suddenly, Lindsey's arousal was through the roof. "Oh my God, that's... Don't stop!" She swallowed, her pulse so fast she feared she'd have a heart attack but, fuck, she didn't care.

Vivian's hand pumped faster, and her pressure and speed on Lindsey's clit increased even more and, oh God, that was it, that was what she needed and—

Lindsey came with a shout, gritting her teeth to keep from howling, although she was dimly aware that probably no one would care if she did. She ground down on Vivian's face, unable to help herself, milking her pleasure for as long as she possibly could. She'd never come so hard in her life, not even touching herself.

This was what sex was all about it, what she'd been missing all this time, and she knew she'd never settle for anything less again.

"Oh, honey." Vivian nuzzled at Lindsey's mound, dropping soft kisses here and there, her hands still holding Lindsey's ass tightly. "Oh, yes."

Lindsey heaved in a huge breath; her heart beat so hard, she was sure Vivian could hear it.

When she released her grip, Vivian gently stroked Lindsey's ass and kissed her belly before standing. She helped Lindsey pull up her clothes, and once the jeans were done up, Vivian pressed her body to her and wrapped her arms around her. When they kissed, Lindsey could taste herself on Vivian's lips and was astonished at how much the flavour and scent stirred a different kind of need in her.

"How are you doing?" Vivian asked when she pulled back.

"Amazing," Lindsey managed to whisper.

Vivian smiled. "I thought so."

Lindsey laughed. "Yes, you can pat yourself on the back."

"Oh, I will." She pinched Lindsey's ass.

"Ow!"

They laughed.

"How's your energy level?" There was an intriguing glint in Vivian's eyes.

She had some aches in unusual places, but generally the euphoria of her orgasm had given her body a wonderful lassitude that didn't seem to want to diminish any time soon. She wasn't sure of the drift of Vivian's question. "Pretty good. Why?"

"Because." Vivian kissed her, still hard and demanding. "Doing that to you has got me all worked up again. I would very much appreciate it," she said with a smirk, "if you'd help an old woman out once more."

Lindsey nodded slowly. "Ah, I see." She loved how playful this woman was. "Well, I'm sure *something* can be arranged." She swallowed. "In fact, I'd love it if…if I could do that to you. Lick you, I mean." Because, oh God yes, she wanted to know what a woman tasted like, what it would feel like to lick all those places. To make Vivian come apart just the way she had done so only minutes before.

The intensity of Vivian's gaze took her breath away. "Are you sure?"

"One hundred percent."

Vivian spun them around so that she was now leaning against the wall, then shoved her own jeans and underwear down, wriggling until they hit her ankles. She opened her legs and placed her hands on Lindsey's shoulders. "Ready when you are, sweetheart."

She pressed gently on Lindsey's shoulders, and that was all the hint Lindsey needed.

Heart thudding once more, she carefully knelt at Vivian's feet. *I'm on my knees in front of a stranger, about to lick her pussy, and nothing has ever felt more right in my life.*

"If you don't like it, stop," Vivian said quietly. "Don't ever do something you don't want, okay?"

"Okay. But I doubt I'm going to be stopping anything for a while."

Vivian smiled.

Lindsey dropped her gaze to the sight before her. Vivian's pubic hair was neatly trimmed and shaved into a petite triangle that left her outer lips bare. They were swollen with her arousal, and the scent of her juices was intoxicating. Sweet and heady, it made Lindsey's mouth water at the prospect of tasting her.

So she wasted no time in doing so. As she dragged her mouth over Vivian's outer labia, and that first tangy taste hit her tongue, her knees almost buckled. "Fuck, that's incredible," she said against Vivian's flesh.

"Oh, yes," came the breathy response from above her.

The power of her situation rushed through her. Vivian was already in delicious turmoil at her touch, and Lindsey only wanted to give her more. She bent her head and used the flat of her tongue to lick the entire length of Vivian's cunt. It was hot and messy and so sexy that it made her own cunt start clenching again. She gripped Vivian's thighs, revelling in the sounds that this woman made, in the thrust of her hips, in the dirty words that fell from her lips.

Lindsey took her time, yet was mindful of Vivian's need, her obvious rising desire and building arousal. Vivian's hands became frantic on Lindsey's shoulders the more Lindsey delved into the folds of Vivian's pussy. She could have spent many happy hours exploring and tasting, but she knew Vivian was close, and it was the least she could do to help the woman come. She lapped up to Vivian's clit, the shaft of it long and swollen, the head hard and so easy to latch onto with her lips.

"Oh, fuck, yes!" Vivian cried, pushing her hips forward, forcing her clit deeper between Lindsey's lips.

Lindsey sucked and licked, determined to give her absolute best to Vivian, to show her just how much everything they'd shared tonight, how much Vivian had taught her, meant to her. She buried her face deeper, loving how her chin and face were smeared with Vivian's arousal, how much Vivian bucked against her as she did so.

And then, after a few more hard and fast licks against that beautifully hard nub, Vivian's thighs trembled in Lindsey's hands and she cried out, humping against Lindsey's face.

Lindsey kept her tongue firm on the clit as Vivian ground against her, aware that her face was a mess of Vivian's juices and her own saliva, and smiling inside at the situation. If someone had told her even a year ago, when she was finalising her divorce, that she'd be here now, like this, she would have thought they were mad.

Vivian squeezed her shoulders. "You can stop now."

Lindsey leaned away from her, licking her lips, loving the taste that still coated her tongue. She helped Vivian pull up her trousers, then stood, wincing a little as her knees complained.

"Sore?" Vivian gave her a sultry smile before dropping a soft kiss on her lips.

"Yes. But very much worth it."

"Oh, I agree."

Lindsey smiled and kissed Vivian again. "Thank you."

Vivian patted Lindsey's hip. "Likewise." She tilted her head. "How's your confidence level now?" Amusement danced in her eyes.

"Amazing." Lindsey grinned.

"So it should be. You have nothing to worry about, honey. Get on out there. Whichever woman you set your sights on, she's going to be very lucky to have you." Vivian winked once more, then strolled off without another word.

Lindsey watched her go, not feeling sad or deflated that their time had come to an end. Vivian had given her a valuable gift, but she also knew Vivian had got exactly what she needed from it to.

Oh yes, she certainly did.

Lindsey grinned as she headed towards the toilets to get cleaned up. *I made a woman come! Twice!*

She strode across the darkened room, her head high, her blood singing in her veins.

CHAPTER 3

LAURA

Mandy's hands shook a little as she stared at the green-eyed woman in front of her. "That was you that night in Brixton? Oh my God."

The woman smiled and nodded. "I'm Laura." She shook her head. "This is wild. I always wanted to apologise to you for not making sure you got home okay that night. And now I can." Her smile widened. "I don't remember your name, but I'm sorry for abandoning you."

Mandy laughed. Her heart beat just a tad faster than normal, but she didn't know why. "It's Mandy. And hey, come on, no apology necessary. That was a crazy scene that night, but we were okay."

"Good, I'm glad. I always wondered."

The door buzzer sounded before Mandy could respond.

"I'll get that." Dee stood in the office doorway to Mandy's right. "Why don't you guys come in here?" She gestured to the office behind her.

"Oh, yeah. That's…thanks." *Why am I so flustered?* Mandy shuffled around Dee, leaving her free to get to the door, and motioned for Laura to follow her into the office.

The sounds of their next visitors being greeted drifted through the doorway, but Mandy found she couldn't pay attention. Her gaze was drawn once more to this woman from her past.

Laura was still an attractive woman, although Mandy had to admit she could barely remember what she'd looked like back then. The bleached-blonde hair seemed vaguely familiar, but that was all. But no matter the past, the woman stood before her now was very easy on the eye.

"So, this place is yours?" Laura glanced around the office and gestured with one hand to encompass all she couldn't see.

"It is." Mandy's voice croaked; she cleared her throat. "We opened eighteen months ago."

"That's great." Laura ran a hand through the back of her hair, and Mandy noticed the strength in her fingers, the creases and scars that dotted the back of her hand, which spoke of some kind of manual work in Laura's past or present. "I always wanted a place like this to exist back in the day. You know, back when we…" She blushed.

Mandy's own cheeks warmed, much to her surprise. Yes, the last time she had been in Laura's presence, Laura had only minutes before had two fingers buried deep inside Mandy. *This is so bizarre.* "Yeah, well, those days were the inspiration for this. There were only so many toilets I wanted to fuck in, you know?"

Laura's laugh burst out. "God, yeah." She shuffled her feet. "I looked for you. After that night. Every time I went out to one of the clubs, I was hoping I'd run into you again. Have the chance to apologise, if nothing else. But I never saw you."

"I left the country. I was so fed up with sneaking around, not being able to live as I wanted." Not even Dee knew this about her past. But somehow, meeting a person from that past made it easy to explain. "I worked and partied my way around the world for a few years, learning as much as I could along the way about what places worked and why." She opened her arms. "And here I am."

They stared at each other for a few moments.

"So, you live in Manchester?" Mandy wondered why she hoped the answer would be yes.

"No. Just up for the weekend. I live in Brighton now. Left London when I met—" She took half a step back, her eyes seeming haunted. "Well, I should let you get back to work." Her voice was rough.

"I suppose so. And I should let you get on and enjoy your evening." She stood up straighter and switched into full business mode. "Do you know much about how the club works and what to expect?"

As part of Laura listened to Mandy explaining the basic premise of the three rooms she could explore at the club, the rest of her was mesmerised by those blue eyes, by the confidence Mandy exuded, and by the soft curves of her figure. She had longer hair than Laura remembered. Of course, its mid-brown colour was now shot through with grey, but the loose, slightly shaggy style suited her.

Mandy was maybe three or four years older than her. Like Laura, her figure had softened with age, but she wore it well. She also looked incredible in the black dress pants and dark blue, open-necked shirt she wore tucked into them. Small diamond earrings, two pairs in each ear, were her only jewellery. She exuded a casual classiness that was ridiculously attractive.

"All okay?" Mandy tilted her head.

Embarrassed at being caught staring, Laura nodded sharply. "Yeah, all good. Twenty quid, yes?"

"That's right." Mandy's eyes sparkled. "Sorry, no mates' rates."

Laura laughed. "No worries." She dug in her wallet for a twenty and handed it over.

The money was tucked into a cashbox on the desk. "Need a locker for your jacket?"

"That would be great." Laura followed her down a dim hallway to a small room lined with lockers and pocketed the key once her jacket was safely stowed away.

"Well." Mandy gestured to the door at the end of the hallway. "Enjoy your evening." Her gaze met Laura's, then flitted away.

"Yeah, uh, thanks." *Okay, now this feels really weird.* "It was…it was good to see you again."

"And you." Mandy flushed a little and took a step back.

Laura wanted to say something but had no idea what. Somehow, the thought of stepping through the door into the heart of the club to find whatever excitement awaited her no longer held the same appeal as it had on the doorstep some fifteen minutes before. Strangely, all she wanted to do now was sit down with Mandy and talk, reminisce some, find out more about how Mandy had come to own this club.

Don't be ridiculous. You barely know the woman! And Mandy had a business to run. She threw Mandy a smile and walked away.

The door from the hallway opened into a short passage that led to what Mandy had called the Green Room. While the lighting was dim, there was enough illumination to see that the room held at least twenty women, some of whom were already coupled up and hard at work along the walls and in the far corners.

Laura stood still for a moment, letting her eyes adjust to the new light level, then breathed in deeply before striding over to the bar. Maybe a drink would help, take her mind off her unexpected meeting just now.

"Hi, what can I get you?" The woman behind the bar had blonde curls which bounced as she moved and a welcoming smile.

"A white wine, if you have it." Laura eased onto the tall stool at the far end of the bar; the seat gave her the best view of the room.

"Sure thing."

A minute later, a chilled glass of wine was placed next to Laura's elbow. After she'd paid, she swivelled in her seat to take in her surroundings. A high table stood in the centre of the room and a few women sat along its length, also watching the events round them. Some of the women seemed to be together, while the rest were clearly on their own.

She let her gaze roam. Cool music piped in from somewhere. Despite her strange mood following the interaction with Mandy, she couldn't help but be aroused by everything around her. A couple to her left were fucking each other, if her eyesight didn't fail her. The rhythm they set, the familiar in and out motion of their moving hands, stirred a longing in her that surprised her with its intensity.

As she sipped her wine, her face warmed the longer she stared at the couple. Was it okay to watch like this? To stare so openly? She looked around. Well, everyone else was watching someone just as intently as she was.

The couple ramped up their energy, their cries of ecstasy spilling into the room and causing hot and cold shivers to break out all over Laura's body. Her breathing had quickened in pace; she took a long slug of her wine to cool down. *Okay, good. Not dead yet, as suspected.*

She turned her attention to the rest of the room. There were four women leaning casually against the walls in various spots. Mandy had said leaning against a wall signalled your availability. *Could I do that? Just send that message out there?*

Not likely. What if no one gave her a second glance? No, if she was going to do anything, she'd have to be the one taking charge.

Yeah, that's how she'd played in the past, always being the one to step forward, to make the first move—like she'd done with Mandy that night back in Brixton.

The memory was stronger than she expected—it was those damn eyes of Mandy's. They'd pulled at her from across that dance floor back then, and with the way she moved her body to the music, it had been a no-brainer to stride over there, slip her arms around her and start grinding out the beat together—and, a few minutes later, to dip her head and kiss her, taste those full lips and know what that mouth felt like pressed against hers.

Come on, you're not here to look back. Tonight was supposed to be about moving on, looking ahead, about leaving the past behind. And, if it were possible, all the hurt.

Could she do it? Could she walk across the room, pick some cute thing and just get at it? The last woman she'd touched had been Kelly, over four years ago. They'd been so good together in bed. She'd never imagined then she'd be thinking one day about getting physical with someone else than her wife. Kelly's death had sent Laura's life on a path she didn't remotely want but had to walk anyway.

She couldn't ignore what her body had been telling her for a few months though. Or what it told her now, watching the women around her fuck at will. She thought about the hot kiss she'd seen in a lesbian romantic comedy on Netflix a few months previously and how the guilt had gnawed at her, as if she were betraying Kelly somehow by being aroused by it. But life had to go on, didn't it?

So here she was. This club was the best way to test out those desires—and those feelings of guilt—without risking her heart or anyone else's.

There was one spare stool at the centre table, so she claimed it quickly. The room had filled up while she'd mused at the bar, and she found herself pleased for Mandy that she'd created such a popular space. Good for her with going through with it.

She wondered if Mandy had a partner, either in the business or in life. That tall blonde in the office? Nah. Somehow, that didn't fit. *Wonder what her type is?* If she did have a life partner, what did they think of her running such a place? And if she didn't, did that mean she indulged here in the club whenever she felt the urge?

Okay, wait, why are you thinking about Mandy?

She inhaled deeply, then let her breath out slowly. Focus. She swept her gaze around the room. Too tall. Too skinny. Too young. Too redheaded.

She wanted to roll her eyes. *What are you, Goldilocks?* Surely anyone who looked nothing like Kelly would be good enough to not fuck with her mind, right?

Yeah, but I at least have to find them physically attractive, don't I?

To her left, someone walked into the main part of the room from the bar area, and Laura sat up a little in her seat. *Wow.* The newcomer was blonde, and the soft lighting in the ceiling picked out the highlights in her long hair, giving it the look of a golden halo around her head. She was curvaceous in a way that reminded Laura of those glamorous movie stars from the fifties and sixties. And she wore a dress which clung to all those curves. The top cut low into her cleavage with the thin straps probably working overtime to keep the whole thing up.

Please stay in this room, Laura found herself mentally chanting. *And please go lean up against a wall.* Vaguely, she noted that she now seemed to have no doubts about what she would do, given the chance. Clearly it had just needed someone with the right looks to banish her remaining doubts. She hadn't thought she was that shallow a person, not generally, but these were special circumstances, after all.

As soon as the blonde took up a spot at the wall towards the right side of the room, Laura strode across to meet her, single-minded in her purpose, her head held high. It almost felt like the old days, and that gave her even more confidence.

"Hi," the blonde said as Laura reached her.

"Hi yourself." Laura smiled at her. Inside, she quivered, but she hoped it didn't show in her expression.

The woman looked her up and down. "What's your name?"

Well, okay. Clearly, she'd seen something she liked. Laura's spine straightened even further. "Laura. You?"

"Toni."

Laura stared into her hazel eyes, then let her gaze roam over Toni's flawless skin, the pert little nose, the small dimple in the centre of her chin. She was perhaps in her mid-thirties, so at least not so young that Laura would feel odd about the age gap between them.

Toni let out a breath, then caught her bottom lip between her teeth. That lip was plump, deep pink with lipstick. The way Toni tugged on it sent a spike of desire rushing straight to Laura's clit.

It made her breath catch.

"What do you want?" Toni asked into the charged silence between them, her voice low and a little husky.

"I want…skin and to…feel you." Words weren't coming easily, but Toni's hum of pleasure told Laura she didn't need to worry.

She placed her hands on Toni's waist; warmth met her fingertips and seared through her.

Toni wet her lips.

Another wave of desire washed through Laura. Those lips looked so tempting. She'd thought kissing would be off the table tonight. Too intimate, personal. But looking at Toni's lips now, she wondered: would it feel that odd?

Toni kissed her, her lips tender but eager, and Laura didn't know whether to freeze or melt. The next moment, her body made it very clear she was overthinking everything, and she sank into Toni's caress. She placed her hands flat on the small of the woman's back and tugged her in closer. When Toni's hand cupped the back of her neck, pressing their mouths tight together, she surrendered to the hot wetness of that luscious mouth and parted her own lips.

The heat engendered by their tongues touching, then stroking, nearly made her knees buckle. Yes, kissing was an intimate thing, and yes, kissing a stranger in a darkened club full of anonymous people didn't compare to kissing the woman she'd loved and married. But in this moment, with want aching through her pussy, Laura didn't care. Demons were being exorcised with every second, and she welcomed it.

Toni moaned and deepened the kiss when Laura wrapped her arms fully around her, melding their breasts, bellies, and thighs together.

The need inside her climbed to staggering proportions. She was on fire. She yearned to reach inside Toni's dress, cup her breasts, stroke through the wetness she hoped to find between her thighs. She shifted position to bring her thigh between Toni's legs and pushed gently against her. Her reward was a sucked-in breath and Toni's other hand clutching at her bicep.

"I really need to touch your skin." Laura stared into Toni's eyes. "Can I?"

Toni nodded, and before Laura could decide which part of skin she wanted to touch first, she grabbed one of Laura's hands and pulled it down towards the hemline of her dress.

Message received loud and clear. She ran her hand firmly up the bare thigh that awaited her. The warm skin that greeted her was almost softer than the fabric over it, and she groaned at the touch. She swept her hand upwards. A thin wisp of underwear greeted her fingertips, and she enjoyed slipping those same fingertips underneath it. It generated a soft gasp and a shudder.

She ran her hand around Toni's hip, beneath her underwear, and round to cup her ass, stroking and kneading the rounded globe. Toni's curves were sinfully sexy, and although desperation for things far more intimate coursed through Laura's veins, she wanted to enjoy as much of Toni as she could.

She seemed to be of the same mind, thrusting her ass back into Laura's hand. "Love that," she hissed into Laura's ear. "Use both hands."

Laura did, cupping Toni's full behind and alternating soft strokes with firm grabs. She parted the cheeks, which provoked increasingly loud groans. After kissing Toni's neck, she dipped her head to lick across her collarbone, the bare skin of her upper chest, down into her cleavage. The heat there was incredible, the valley created by her breasts deep and enticing.

Thoughts of Kelly's breasts, full and so responsive, threatened to push their way to the forefront, and she almost physically shook her head to send them away. *No, not now.* Now was simply about enjoying being this physical again. It didn't mean anything more than that, and she didn't need to feel guilty about it.

Toni snaked a hand between them and up to one of the dress straps. She slid it off her shoulder and shimmied a little until it dropped past her bicep. She pulled the dress back from her breast, and Laura watched entranced as she let the full mound pop free of the fabric a few tantalising inches from Laura's mouth. A rosy-pink hard nipple stood to attention, signalling Toni's need better than words could.

Laura didn't waste any time answering that call; she bent farther, her hands still clasping Toni's ass, and swiped her tongue over the nipple.

"Fuuuuuck." Toni arched into her, pushing her breast against Laura's face.

She took full advantage, enclosing the nipple and a satisfying portion of breast with her mouth. She sucked hard, then pulled back a little and licked all around the nipple and areola before taking the nipple between her teeth. She didn't bite, merely held.

"Please," Toni begged, her voice a ragged whisper.

Laura bit—gently at first, then increasing the pressure the more Toni writhed against her. Her satisfaction at hearing the effect her touch had on Toni was probably out of proportion to events, but she smiled anyway.

Okay, none of the important stuff forgotten. And she was okay with this. More than okay—a fact which held more meaning. She wanted it, wanted to go further, to see if she could make Toni completely unravel.

She laved her tongue over the nipple, then went back again with her teeth, this time forceful before softening to a gentle nip.

"So good. Don't stop that." Toni looked down at her, and their gazes locked. "But if you want to move your hands to other places, that would also be good." She grinned.

Laura chuckled against Toni's breast but did as the lady asked. She gave her ass cheeks one last deep squeeze, then slid her hands around inside the skimpy underwear to the front of Toni's body. A short fuzz of hair greeted her fingertips along with an exceptional amount of heat. "Mm, someone's hot."

She smiled up at Toni, whose eyes were heavy-lidded with desire. Laura stood, needing a break from the stooped position required to service Toni's breasts.

As soon as she did, Toni lunged for her mouth once more, her kiss hungry and demanding, her tongue pushing deep. Laura answered with equal need, her pussy soaking wet, her clit throbbing against the confines of her tight boy shorts.

With her right hand on Toni's hip, she held the fingertips of her left hand just above Toni's clit, wanting to prolong the moment before she dipped into the wetness she was sure awaited her.

Toni tensed a little, pulling back from the kiss, her breathing heavy. She licked her lips. There was an uncertainty in her eyes that hadn't been there before.

"You okay?" Laura stilled everything in her body and held her gaze. "Want to stop?"

Toni shook her head, licked her lips once more. "No, it's…" Her gaze darted away, and she exhaled deeply. "Can you not…go inside me?" She spoke so quietly, Laura was sure she wouldn't have heard her if they hadn't been pressed so close together.

"Of course." Laura waited until Toni met her eyes once more. "If that's not something you want, I totally respect that."

The relief was obvious, not only in Toni's eyes but in the way her body relaxed, as if a moment before she had been made of steel and now was purely jelly. She shook a little as she leaned in for a soft kiss.

"Hey." Laura pressed a little closer. "You okay?"

Toni nodded, but her blush was obvious even in this dim light. "Yes. I… Everyone always seems to expect it, and I really don't like it. It's always so awkward bringing it up, and sometimes I've had women here get really weird with me about it."

"Jesus." Laura stared at her. "Seriously? God, I'm so sorry about that. You have every right to say what you want or don't want, and anyone who doesn't respect that is an asshole." Coming here, it had never occurred to her that everyone wouldn't be that respectful of each other's wishes. *Christ, how naive of me.*

"Thank you." Toni smiled, then puffed out a breath. "Didn't mean to spoil the moment."

"You didn't." Laura kissed her, a rush of tenderness filling her at the courage of this woman she didn't know. "So, what *do* you like?"

"Well"—Toni wrapped her arms around Laura's shoulders—"I have very sensitive labia, and I love having them stroked."

Laura's entire pussy clenched at the thought.

"And my clit, although a little on the small side, is super sensitive, so if you use some of my wetness to coat it thoroughly before you start rubbing it, that helps to, um, prolong things."

Laura groaned. "Oh my God, you're killing me."

The look of pride on Toni's face was exactly what Laura wanted to see. Given that Toni had not had the best of times here before, it amazed Laura that she was back and willing to try again. She was going to give Toni everything she wanted. Whatever that was, she knew it would completely satisfy her too.

"You'll be killing me too." Toni's expression turned sultry. "If you don't move your fingers soon…"

Smiling, Laura once again gave Toni what she asked for. Spreading her forefinger and middle finger wide, she caressed lightly over Toni's outer labia. The lips were bare, and the softness of them was a delight to her senses.

Toni moaned and her eyelids fluttered shut. "Yes…"

Laura swept equally slowly and lightly back along those same labia until her fingertips hovered once more just above Toni's trimmed pubic hair.

Toni pushed towards her hand.

"More?" Laura teased, licking at Toni's bottom lip before kissing her again.

Toni's hips thrust even harder in the direction of Laura's hand.

"Well, okay, then. If you feel that strongly about it." Laura smirked.

Toni's chuckle transformed into a husky groan as Laura brushed her two fingers down the length of the woman's labia, then dipped quickly into the copious, warm wetness that had pooled between them. She dragged that wetness back with her fingers as she reversed her path, and this time Toni gasped.

"Good?" Laura was determined to regularly check in, something she had been prone to do with Kelly. With what Toni had shared with her, it seemed even more important to do so in this encounter.

"Very." Toni's voice was a rasp against Laura's mouth. "Fuck, I'm so wet."

"Yes, you are. It's fantastic." And it was. Knowing she could make someone feel like this made *her* feel about ten feet tall.

Toni kissed her hard.

She stroked Toni's tongue with her own, stroking her pussy lips at the same time. The smoothness of them, lubricated with Toni's juices, nearly robbed Laura of breath. She coated her fingers with even more fluid, then traced circles and figures of eight over Toni's labia, loving the soft whimpers and moans her actions elicited. When she slid both fingers into the hot, wet channel between the outer and inner labia, both of them groaned into each other's mouths.

"Fuck, that's hot." Laura's voice was a hoarse, desire-filled croak. She was so turned on it was painful. And yet, she knew she still wasn't quite ready to be touched herself. It was easy to gently nudge Toni's hands away when she made to slip them under Laura's shirt. "I'm good," she said, making sure to look into her eyes as she said it. "I just want to touch you, okay?"

Toni pouted, then smiled. "If you're sure."

"Totally." Laura shifted position so she could take her free hand up to Toni's exposed breast. She pinched the nipple, rolling it between her fingers, and then rubbed into Toni's wetness again with the other hand.

Toni's eyes closed as her head tipped back. "Yes. Fuck, *yes*."

Laura began a steady rhythm, rolling the nipple while stroking back and forth through Toni's wet pussy. She kept away from her clit for now, although it was hard to resist. Toni's swollen labia cocooned her fingers in their wet warmth and set her blood racing. She massaged Toni's breast, the fullness of it just enough to fill her hand, the nipple a hard bud pushing into her palm.

"Please, now." Toni's voice was strained, her fingers frantic, as she clasped Laura's hips.

"Now?" Laura prolonged the moment, dipping once more into Toni's wetness, dragging her fingers once more up and down her drenched pussy.

"Oh God, yes!"

Laura watched Toni's face as she moved her fingers up to her clit. Her pleasure was evident; her cheeks had flushed, her eyelids fluttered and her lips stayed parted. She found Toni's clit hard and ready—small, as Toni had said, but standing up eager for some attention.

The sound that escaped Toni's throat as Laura slowly stroked up her clit, then down, was part gasp, part groan. Laura pressed harder, rubbed a little faster, and Toni bucked against her. She moved her fingers even faster, using two pressed flatly against the hard nub to apply even pressure while she upped her pace.

Toni gasped for breath, her lips close to Laura's ear.

The sound spurred Laura on, as did the thrusting of Toni's hips. She briefly left Toni's clit to coat her fingers again, then returned to her mission of making Toni come apart all over her hand. Her fingers were so wet, slipping over Toni with ease, sometimes stroking the hood, sometimes parting and rubbing the sides. Whatever she did, Toni responded with moans and thrusts, but when she pressed more firmly with the flats of her fingers, she knew she'd found exactly the right spot.

Toni sucked in a breath and went rigid in her arms. In the next moment, she let out a low, keening cry. She humped against Laura's hand as her orgasm took hold and pressed her lips to Laura's ear. "Yes. Yes. Yes."

Laura kept up her movement, keeping up the pressure. Her entire body strained with the effort of holding Toni against her, fearing she'd slide down the wall if she didn't. The heat and wetness between Toni's legs seemed to increase tenfold, but that was a burden Laura was happy to bear. She'd never thought she'd experience the feel of a woman coming in her arms again, and certainly not with a complete stranger she'd met only twenty minutes before. That life was supposed to have been gone, and she'd been okay with that.

"You can stop now." Toni's voice was hoarse.

Laura stilled her fingers; she'd tuned Toni out while pondering her own reactions. "Want me to stay there or move away?"

"Away would be good. Super sensitive now."

Laura eased her fingers away from that lovely wet heat, then out of Toni's underwear altogether. She held her hand away from them, not wanting either of them to have to wear the evidence of Toni's pleasure on their clothes.

"That was pretty amazing." Toni leaned in to kiss her. "Thank you."

"You're very welcome. I'm glad I could do that for you." *And for me*. Confirmation her sex life didn't have to be over was gratefully received. The tricky thing would be working out what this meant for her longer term.

More of this? Quick, relatively unemotional encounters in this club? Or use this as a stepping stone to something more meaningful? But that would involve her heart once more, something she really wasn't sure she had the strength for yet.

"Are you sure you're okay? Need anything?" Toni's voice was a mix of sexy come-on and concern.

Laura blinked, then shook her head. "No, honestly. I'm good. That was… Thank you." What could she say? Thanks for letting me blow away the cobwebs? Scratch an itch?

"Well, okay." Toni let go of Laura's hips and straightened slightly. She reached for her dress strap still hanging down around her elbow.

Laura blushed. She still held Toni's breast in her hand. She dropped her hold with a sheepish grin.

Toni chuckled, fixed her dress back into place, then gave Laura a quick peck on her lips. "Thanks. I'm going to wash up now. Enjoy the rest of your night."

The words were said with some warmth, but it was still a dismissal.

Laura backed away and made room for Toni to be able to walk past her. She watched her go, these curvy hips swaying with a natural sass and grace. "Thanks," she murmured after her before flopping against the wall. She'd head to the bathrooms too in a moment, but she'd give Toni some time alone in there first. It would seem even more strange to make small talk as they cleaned up.

She found a tissue in her pocket and cleaned up her fingers as best she could while she waited. Her thoughts buzzed as she replayed what had happened and how it had all made her feel. Satisfied, yes. Relieved too. But also, somehow, strangely empty. Apart from the moment of tenderness she'd felt when assuring Toni it was okay to ask for what she did—and didn't—want, what they'd shared had been quick, physical, enjoyable but singularly lacking in shared emotions. She'd done that many times in the past, and it had been just what she needed…then. Now, twenty years older and wiser, her emotional landscape filled with remembered love and pain, it was easy to see that encounters like tonight's weren't a long-term option.

The club had been good to her for one night, but that was all she wanted.

Mandy drummed her fingers on the desk, then realised what she was doing and snatched her hand away. *You're being ridiculous.*

"You okay?" Dee asked.

"Fine." She reached for her tea but grimaced when she found it cold. Well, at least making a fresh cup would give her something to do and stop her thinking about Laura.

There, she'd admitted it to herself. She was thinking about Laura, and she had no idea why.

After Laura had disappeared into the Green Room, Mandy had taken a moment in the office, waiting for her heated face to cool. Blushing over the haziest memories of a quick fuck with the woman twenty-five years previously was beyond silly. But the last thing she wanted was for Dee to see that blush and think—well, whatever she'd think.

"She someone you know? I haven't seen her here before, and I'm pretty sure I'd remember because she's hot." Dee's tone was playful.

Mandy's blush deepened, and she silently cursed her observant assistant. Then her brain decided to go on a quest down memory lane and see what it could dig up from that night all those years ago.

She spoke before she could think about whether it was a good idea or not. "Yes, Laura and I knew each other many years ago, although only briefly."

Dee grinned. "Yeah?"

Mandy snorted. "All right, I'll tell you. She was the woman I was with the night I got hit by that homophobe. Remember, I told you?"

"Oh yeah! Right, okay, it's all clicking into place now—the thing you said was the last straw for you and London."

"Yes. I never hit the clubs again and left the country a few weeks later."

"And Laura?"

"Well, obviously I never saw her again, although, apparently, she hunted for me in those weeks after, hoping to see I was okay and apologise for not doing more that night."

"Ah, sweet! She sounds nice. Like someone you should get to know again. And you know, she *is* hot." She mimed wiping her brow.

"Shut up."

Dee laughed. "Oh, come on. I saw the way you were looking at her just now."

Mandy scowled. *I'm fifty-five years old. Crushes like this were supposed to have been left behind in my teens.* "I was not." *Oh, good, now I even sound like a teenager.*

"Hey." Dee's voice was soft.

Mandy raised a quizzical eyebrow.

"What would be the harm in it?" She tilted her head. "I saw the way she looked at you too."

"I don't have time for any…entanglements. I run a business that needs all of my attention. You know about Rebecca and how that left me feeling. Never mind the fact that I've never done an actual relationship in my whole life. It's a bit late to start that now, isn't it? So, it doesn't matter how attractive Laura is or how she looks at me."

And she is currently getting down and dirty with someone else only a few metres away. So it was even more silly to think about Laura that way, wasn't it?

"Mandy, at the risk of embarrassing you more, I think you have a lot to offer someone, no matter your past or how busy you think you are now. Because this place does *not* take up all your time. I get that you might be nervous starting over with someone at your age, but if you'd just try…"

Mandy sighed. "It's not that easy." She hadn't told Dee the whole truth, but their friendship didn't run quite deep enough for her to reveal everything about how she was feeling lately.

They looked at each other in silence for a moment, then Dee stood. "I'll leave you alone for a little while. Check on the bars."

Mandy nodded but didn't say anything; her brain was too full of thoughts of the past and how she'd managed her life up this point.

She finished making her tea and returned to her desk. She'd only just sat down when she heard Dee say to someone, "Sure, I'll just see if she's free."

Dee poked her head round the door to the office. Her eyes sparkled with suppressed mirth. "Laura's wondering if you have a minute to chat."

Mandy swallowed and admonished her heart for beating so fast. She stood, straightened her shirt, and walked to the door.

Laura hovered in the hallway, away from the front door, her hands tucked into her jacket pockets.

Oh, leaving so soon? Did that mean she hadn't…?

"Hey." Laura gave Mandy a small, nervous smile.

"Hello, again." Mandy smiled back; she couldn't help it, even as her rational brain wondered why she wasn't being professional and aloof. She motioned for Laura to join her in the office. "So, um, how was your evening?"

Laura's blush was sweet and told Mandy everything she needed to know. Irritation spiked in her at the flicker of jealousy curling in her belly.

"It's a great club. You should be really proud of yourself." Laura pulled her hands from her pockets and meshed her fingers together, twisting and turning them.

"I am." Mandy smiled. "I'm glad you like it." She was, no matter her irrational reaction to Laura actually enjoying herself here.

"Listen." Laura took one step forward, her gaze darting away then back again. "I don't know if this will sound a bit odd, but…" She licked her lips. "I'm here all weekend, and I wondered if you maybe fancied meeting for lunch, or just a coffee, tomorrow? If you have time? I'd love to catch up, talk with someone from the old days and all that." Her hands twisted even more fervently in front of her.

If she said no, that would be the end of it. It was highly unlikely Laura would return, and even if she did, it would be purely as a punter. She'd probably never see Laura again, and she could forget all about these strange feelings seeing her tonight had produced.

"Yes, but..." she could imagine Dee saying. *"What if?"*

Mandy had never yearned for a relationship as her acquaintances did. She'd never been into all the hearts and flowers romantic stuff, or even the idea of monogamy—except when she'd fallen in love with the unattainable Rebecca. But somehow, in her fifties, after the heartbreak of losing Rebecca, she'd found herself sometimes wondering what it would be like to actually date someone. To learn about a new person and discover what kind of woman she would fit with, could perhaps build something with. Share more than just sex with.

It was odd that—as the owner of a club offering women the opportunity to indulge in just sex with anyone they wanted, any way they wanted—she should suddenly be shying away from that for herself. But she'd also been someone who'd always listened to her body and her needs. And lately, her body—and soul, for want of a better word—had been telling her she was lonely, no matter what half-truths she'd told Dee only minutes before.

"I think lunch sounds like a great idea." She smiled when Laura's eyes widened in surprise. "I know a great place, if you don't mind me recommending?"

"Not at all." Laura cleared her throat, and finally a smile graced her lips. "Just say when and where and I'll be there, ready and willing."

It was so wrong that those eager words conjured up all sorts of possibilities in Mandy's head that had nothing to do with lunch.

Wasn't it?

CHAPTER 4

CAITLIN

CAITLIN SAVED THE DOCUMENT AND closed down her computer. Done for the day. She leaned back and stretched her arms high above her head, hearing the satisfying pop of her vertebrae as they realigned after the long afternoon stuck at her desk.

Across the office from her, her two assistants stood and began packing up their bags, waving and calling out for Caitlin to have a nice weekend as they departed.

Her boss was on the phone in her office as Caitlin left. She also threw Caitlin a wave and a mouthed, "See you Monday" as Caitlin walked by her open door.

Thank God. Often on Fridays Zoe would want to digest the day before Caitlin left, running through the calendar for the week ahead, checking where each van was right now and when it was due back. Caitlin did love her work at the removals firm, even though it was a far cry from what she thought she'd end up doing when she left college, but she wasn't in the mood for work talk tonight. It was the middle of summer, a beautiful evening, and she fancied a glass of wine on her tiny balcony before the sun set.

She took the lift down to the ground floor and headed out the back door to the staff car park. As she turned to the left to where her car was parked, Kris, the gorgeous androgynous woman who'd joined the company last year as an additional driver-mover came from the other direction, swirling some truck keys in her hand.

"Oh, hey, Caitlin," Kris said, giving her one of those beaming smiles she excelled at.

Caitlin glowed in the heat of it. "Hi."

"Off home?"

"Yes. You too?"

"Nearly. Just need to collect the paperwork for that early morning job tomorrow."

"Ah, yes!" *Go on, ask her! You've been wanting to do it for ages.* Her interest in Kris had only grown the more they interacted, and this evening she looked delectable in dungarees over a white company T-shirt, her Dr Martens scuffed and rugged on her feet. And their easy flirting had gone on for a few weeks now.

So come on. Ask her!

Kris walked past her. "See you in the morning."

"Hey, Kris?" Caitlin's heart pounded.

Kris turned back to her. "Yeah?"

"I was, um, wondering. Do you fancy meeting for a drink one night? Maybe tomorrow?"

Kris's eyes widened, and she dug at the ground with the toe of one of her boots. "Oh. Sorry, no. Appreciate you putting yourself out there, but no thanks."

Caitlin's stomach sank to her knees. "Oh. Oh, right. Okay, have a nice night." She scurried away towards her car, cheeks blazing with heat. Fuck! She'd been so sure. So sure she'd read all the signs. Fuck.

If only Kris wasn't everything Caitlin had come to realise she admired in another woman—tall, strong, short hair, butch, cool dress sense. Yep, Kris had it all, and Caitlin had wanted it all, badly, ever since Kris had first started working for them. She'd let herself get carried away, wondering if, finally, she'd found a woman who could meet all her needs.

Still swearing under her breath, she reached her car, unlocked it, and got in. She was about to put the car in gear, desperate to get out of the car park and away from Kris, when her phone chimed.

On the screen was a Facebook notification from a queer kink group she'd joined only a couple of months ago. She still wasn't sure if the group was a good fit for her, so up until now she'd kept a low profile in there, merely watching rather than participating. But she'd set up notifications for new events, just in case anything that might appeal hit her radar. She would have put the phone back in her bag, but the preview of the notification snagged her attention.

Women-only sex club! Every Friday and Saturday, Manchester, 9pm till late.

Without hesitating, she swiped to open the full post and read it quickly. Then she read it again, her heart rate increasing, her mind whirling. Suddenly all thoughts of Kris had vanished.

Mandy laughed as Nina teased Dee's two-finger typing style.

"Come on, Dee, we're practically the same age! How come you can't type quicker than this?" Nina shook her head.

"Fuck off, you little runt." Dee glowered at Nina, but her smirk was playful.

The two of them had been like that with each other as long as they'd both been working at the club, but now that Dee was training Nina up as her replacement, their banter had elevated to a new level.

"Come on, help me out here, Mandy." Nina met her gaze, her eyes sparkling. "It'll take weeks to train me at this rate."

Mandy shook her head. "It won't, and you know it. Leave her be. She's done more than okay while she's been in charge of those spreadsheets. Learn from the master and be quiet about it."

"Hah!" Dee stood up, grinning from ear to ear, and motioned Nina to take her seat in front of the computer. "Hear that? I'm the master. You are the young apprentice. Deal with it."

"Whatever." Nina smirked, swished her long dark hair away from her face, and took her seat. "So, anyway," she pointed at the computer screen, "what's this box for?"

Dee bent her head again and they were instantly back to serious training mode, just as Mandy knew they would be. They liked to joke around, but she knew they were both totally dedicated to this handover—and to her club. She was proud of them both for the effort they were making, and the support she'd had from them ever since the club opened.

The office phone rang on one of the internal lines, and Dee punched the speakerphone button by way of answering. "Hey, what's up?"

"Hey, Dee, it's Cassie. I'm out of fivers. Can someone bring me a wad up?"

"I suppose you'd like that someone to have long, black hair and lipstick?" Dee smirked at Nina, who rolled her eyes.

Mandy chuckled. "I'll go. I need to do my rounds anyway." She looked at Nina, a smirk hovering on her lips. "Assuming you don't mind, Nina, dear?"

On the line, Cassie laughed just as Nina snorted.

"We do live together," Nina said, trying for some acid in her tone at the grin on Dee's face and failing miserably. "I can wait until later to see her, you know."

"Oh, Cassie, I think you've lost your charms." Dee laughed.

"Trust me, I haven't," Cassie said, a touch of throatiness in her tone.

Mandy laughed out loud. "Good for you! I'll still be along in a couple of minutes."

"Thanks." Cassie hung up.

"You're such a dick sometimes." Nina shoved Dee's bicep, but she also laughed.

Mandy's heart twinged with a mix of sadness and joy. Dee would leave soon, and that was still a thought that took some getting used to. But Nina was definitely ready to step into her shoes, and Mandy looked forward to working with her more closely.

She strolled out of the office with the required cash in her trouser pocket, and headed for Red, where Cassie was behind bar, as she was nearly every Saturday night. Mandy's heart lifted—her club was in good hands, and that was all that counted.

Caitlin stepped through the open door and into a dimly lit hallway. Her mouth was so dry, she wondered if she'd be able to speak to the dark-haired woman who'd shown her in.

"Hi, and welcome," the woman said. "I'm Nina, the assistant manager here. Welcome to the club."

"Thanks." The word came out as an embarrassing squeak and Caitlin grimaced.

Nina smiled. "Have you been here before?"

Caitlin shook her head, gazing around at the nondescript surroundings. They stood just inside the front door at the start of a long hallway. A few doors led off the left side, as well as one at the end. She couldn't hear a sound from anywhere else and wondered just how big this place was. The event ad in the Facebook group had mentioned three rooms, each with a specific focus. She already knew which room she'd be heading for. The thought made her shiver with thrilled anticipation.

"No, I'm new here." At last, her voice sounded normal. "But I did see some details in a Facebook ad, so I know roughly what's on offer."

She didn't mention that it had been three weeks since she'd seen the ad and that it had taken her that long to pluck up courage to give this a try. Sex with a stranger wasn't high on her fantasy list, but this place offered a whole room full of women interested in what Caitlin was after, and that *was* high on her list. Maybe this was the perfect way to try out her fantasy and see if it really was everything she'd dreamed it would be. Then maybe she'd have more confidence in finding a partner who wanted that as part of their sex life as much as she did.

"Great! But as you're new, I just need to make a couple of things clear, okay?" Nina's smile was still warm, but it was clear she was all business. "We have some pretty simple rules in place for your safety and that of our other clients. Sitting at the bar or one of the high tables in the centre of each room is considered a safe space. There's no touching there and no initiations of any activity, okay?"

"Got it."

"If you want to initiate activity, you find a spot along the wall. That signals your consent to be approached. However, it does not signify consent per se. You are still free to decline anything anyone asks, and they should respect that."

"What if they don't?" Fears of being forced into something she really didn't want, just because everyone thought anything was allowed in a place like this, twisted her stomach into knots.

"Approach the bartender or find your way to the table in the centre of the room." Nina pursed her lipsticked lips. "We can't guarantee everyone here will play by the rules, but, honestly, in all the time we've been open, we've only had to eject two women. And each time, they were drunk and obnoxious rather than dangerous."

Caitlin's tension eased. "Okay. Cool."

"So, still interested?"

"Yes." Caitlin spoke without hesitation, and excitement tingled through her limbs.

"Good! Then I just need to take some money from you and your evening can begin."

After paying, Caitlin took a deep breath and opened the door at the end of the hallway.

The first of the club's three playrooms greeted her—the Green Room—and she spotted the door to the Blue Room as soon as she turned the corner from the bar. Caitlin walked across the room towards the door with the blue light above it, but her pace slowed the farther she got inside the Green Room. Her attention was drawn to what was happening around her.

Wow.

To her right, a tall redhead had her head thrown back against the wall, her skirt pushed up and clutched in her hands at her waist. Her face was contorted in ecstasy as a dark-haired woman knelt before her, licking her.

Next to them, two women in jeans and T-shirts were entwined, kissing deeply, their hands roaming over each other's breasts.

Beyond them, a couple fucked each other, their jeans shoved down to their knees, their cries of pleasure loud enough to reach Caitlin's ears.

Holy shit. She swallowed hard, every hair on her body standing on end as arousal flooded her. It had been about nine months since she'd last had sex. Not that long, really, in the grand scheme of things, but it suddenly felt as if it had been years. Her body yearned to be touched. Her lips burned to be kissed. She wanted to feel what those women felt, that all-encompassing joy and thrill of intimacy with another woman. But she also wanted to live out her fantasy—and for that, she needed to move on from the delicious views around her.

She wrenched her gaze away and opened the door to the Blue Room.

A short hallway led her away from the door, leaving the sounds of the Green Room behind her. Low lights along the edge of the floor guided her to a sharp left turn into the main part of the room. The bar faced her and to her right she could see the high table at the centre of the room. Beyond that, nothing much else was revealed; the lighting in here seemed lower than in the Green Room.

With the combination of nerves and excitement she'd experienced since before arriving at the club, she was parched, so she headed for the bar. A red-headed bartender served her request for an ice-cold beer with alacrity.

Taking a deep breath, Caitlin picked it up and walked over to the high table.

She took a stool towards the left end. To her right, a couple of stools away, two femme women who seemed to know each other chatted and sipped from glasses of wine while they watched the room. At the farthest end of the table sat a lone woman, short-haired, dressed in a white shirt. Cufflinks caught the light when she lifted her beer to her mouth. Caitlin had always loved seeing cufflinks on a woman, and she smiled at the sight.

The first mouthful of beer helped to calm her nerves. As she swallowed, she pulled her gaze away from contemplation of her table companions and looked around the room.

It wasn't as busy in here as in the Green Room, but there were still half a dozen couples in action. Caitlin noticed more chairs in this room as well as some long, low, padded benches. All sorts of ideas swirled through her head at what she and a partner could get up to using one of those.

Her cunt clenched with a sharp flush of arousal, and she grabbed for her beer once more. God knew she wanted the things she'd long fantasised about, but now that she was here, and even knowing how this club worked—how the hell did she find someone who wanted to do all of it too? It wasn't as if she could go around the room asking.

Hey, oh, excuse me, I'm just doing a survey and…

She rolled her eyes. Fuck, she hadn't thought about this bit. Did she just have to figure out which of the available women in the room were packing, and then what, just stroll up and ask? Or should she find her spot against the wall and wait? She wondered if the women who packed preferred to do the asking, to be the more dominant partner. Did it work that way?

Well, there's only one way to find out. And if it didn't work, she could just leave. Her hand trembled slightly as she picked up her beer. She eased off the stool, holding her head high even though her entire body shook with nerves, and walked to a large gap on the left-hand wall.

Her chosen spot positioned her between a chair on one side and a bench on the other. A small shelf in an alcove at shoulder height was a perfect spot for her beer, and after carefully placing the bottle there, she sucked in a breath and turned.

She had to lean her whole weight against the wall, afraid her knees would give way if she didn't.

You have every right to be here. You have every right to want this.

It was the mantra she'd been practising all week as past hurtful comments had returned to haunt her again and again. She'd read some more of her erotica collection during the week too, reaffirming she wasn't alone in wanting the kind of play she desired.

After a couple of deep breaths, she smoothed down her skirt once more. She'd debated what to wear for the evening and had finally settled on a thin, pale pink, low-cut top to show off two of her best assets, and a black, silky skirt that could be pushed up for easy access.

Movement caught her eye; the woman with the white shirt and cufflinks walked away from the centre table. Then she turned and headed in Caitlin's direction.

Caitlin's breath caught. The woman was tall and lithe; her shirt fitted her like a second skin, and she wore it tucked into dark-coloured trousers that hugged her narrow hips. Her short hair, maybe light brown or dark blonde—it was hard to tell at a distance—was cut in a way that perfectly suited her chiselled features. She had a grace about her that was mesmerising.

And she is definitely walking towards me.

Caitlin swallowed and stood up a little straighter, even though her knees still threatened to give way.

The woman drew nearer, and Caitlin couldn't help it—she dropped her gaze to the woman's groin. Even in the dim light, the bulge there was obvious.

Caitlin's mouth went dry.

"Hey." The woman stood maybe a metre away. "Are you interested in having some fun?"

"I…I am." Caitlin licked her lips. "Yes."

The woman smiled, her full lips almost seeming out of place on such a narrow face. "Good. My name's Jas. What's yours?"

"Caitlin." She cleared her throat. "What, um, what are you looking for?" Might as well have the conversation up front. Like Nina had said, it was okay to decline.

Jas stepped closer, her gaze raking Caitlin's body. The heat in that look made her shiver. "Well, I'm someone who prefers to give a woman what *she* wants. Especially a woman as hot as you. Whatever you want from me, I can pretty much guarantee I'll be happy to give it."

Her voice was low and deep, and she spoke with a confidence Caitlin just knew came from her being very comfortable with who she was and what her sexual desires and needs were. It was a huge turn-on in itself.

"I want to suck you." The words shot from her mouth, her voice shaky. "On my knees in front of you. And then I want to straddle you on that bench and ride your cock as hard as I can."

Her cheeks burned, but she wouldn't take back the true words, not for anything.

Jas tilted her head. "Yeah? You seem a little…nervous asking. Are you sure that's what you want?"

"Yes. I am." Caitlin swallowed. "It's just, I had a girlfriend once who said… Well, she said I wasn't a real lesbian if I wanted that. That there was something wrong with me for having those desires. She made me feel really ashamed for the way I feel." Shit, it still hurt, even though it had been nearly two years since Sam had walked out on her after she'd confessed her fantasy.

Jas's mouth set in a grim line. "Well, she sounds charming." She stepped closer. "There's nothing wrong with what you desire. Look around this room. You're not alone in wanting that." She cupped Caitlin's chin. "And nobody gets to dictate your sexuality to you."

Held captive by the fierceness in Jas's eyes, the warmth of her fingers on her face, Caitlin nodded. "Thank you. It's been hard to let those words go and be okay with who I am. With what I want."

"Well, I, for one, am very okay with what you want. You have no idea how wet I got with you telling me just now."

"Really?" Caitlin's heart pounded. "You—you would want to do that with me?"

The sound Jas made then could only be described as a growl. She nodded and closed the distance between them. "Whatever you want, Caitlin."

Caitlin's entire body turned molten at the sound of her name falling from Jas's lips.

Jas placed her hands on the wall either side of Caitlin's head. The action brought her body within range, but it wasn't touching Caitlin's. Yet. "I'd love to start things off with a kiss.

Get a little preview of what your tongue can do. Okay?" Her breath, holding a hint of beer, was warm across Caitlin's lips, her eyes a golden-brown colour that almost glowed like a tiger's eyes in the low light.

Whimpering, Caitlin grabbed hold of Jas's hips. She pulled her in close, her eyes shuttering closed at the feel of Jas's cock pressed between them. Wetness flooded her panties; her cunt already ached to be filled.

Jas's kiss was hard, but Caitlin welcomed it; she burned with need, and softness wouldn't cut it.

She opened her mouth as soon as Jas demanded it, and when their tongues met, she pushed herself even tighter against Jas's lean body. She ran her hands up Jas's back, the crisp cotton of the shirt smooth under her fingertips, the material warm from Jas's body heat.

When Jas thrust against her slightly, the motion made them both groan into each other's mouths. She massaged Caitlin's breasts through the fabric of her flimsy top, and Caitlin couldn't press close enough to have more of that rough treatment.

Jas pulled away, staring into Caitlin's eyes. "That's a very hot mouth you have. I think you ought to show me what else you can do with it."

Oh God, I'm going to come in about thirty seconds if she keeps talking like that. Caitlin's skin was on fire, her pussy throbbing.

When Jas stepped back, Caitlin instantly felt adrift. Then Jas reached into the back pocket of her trousers and pulled out a couple of condoms.

Caitlin's brain froze. *I'm actually going to do this. Holy shit.*

"Strawberry or mint?" Jas smirked.

Caitlin's laugh burst out. Her nerves tamped down a bit. "I'll try the mint one."

Jas held Caitlin's gaze as she put the other condom back in her pocket. Then her expression turned serious, and her eyes a shade darker. "On your knees."

Sure she was wetter than she'd ever been in her life, Caitlin dropped to her knees. The fake wood floor was hard against her skin, but she didn't care—she'd wear any bruises with fond memories of how they were obtained. Then her gaze was drawn away from contemplation of her situation and back to Jas's hands.

Jas unzipped her trousers and eased them open. Underneath, she wore tight black briefs that were clearly tailor-made for wearing a dildo, with a reinforced O ring in the middle of the material. And released now from its confines of the trousers was her dildo, jutting out from the trousers' opening.

Caitlin swallowed. It was bigger than she'd been expecting. Maybe seven inches long, about an inch and a half wide at the base. It tapered slightly to its rounded end, and she was pleased that it wasn't one of those too-realistic ones, nor was it flesh-coloured. The purple shade was actually kind of funky.

She took in the length of it again as Jas rolled on the condom. *Can I take this? Either in my mouth or my pussy?* Her mouth had gone dry once more, and she rolled her tongue a little to free things up.

Jas's hand on her head stilled her. "You okay? Still want to do this?"

"Yes. Thanks for checking in, but I'm okay." She paused, then plunged on. "I've fantasised about this for years but never actually done it."

Jas's smile was understanding. "I wondered." She stroked Caitlin's cheek. "Go at your pace. Whatever you need, remember? With that hot mouth of yours, I know I'm going to love whatever you do."

"Fuck." Caitlin shuddered. "The way you talk..." She dropped her gaze to Jas's cock, which Jas held lightly in one hand. "I want to suck you so bad."

"Oh, fuck. Yes." Jas gazed down at her. "Do it. Suck me."

Caitlin leaned forward and placed her hands on the sides of Jas's thighs for balance. The dildo was now directly in front of her face, held steady by Jas. Caitlin licked her lips and opened her mouth.

Jas groaned above her.

Caitlin wrapped her lips around Jas's cock and took it into her mouth. It filled her, but the sensation wasn't scary or uncomfortable. She took her deeper, wetting the length of it as much as she could with her saliva, letting her tongue swirl around it as far as was possible. *Jesus, this feels amazing.*

On her knees, her mouth full of dildo, the woman she sucked off obviously enjoying herself, Caitlin suddenly felt on top of the world. Some fantasies were totally worth pursuing, clearly. *And screw anyone who says I'm wrong to want this. When it feels this amazing, there's no way I'm not going to do it.*

"Oh, fuck. That looks so good. Feels so good." Jas stared down at her, her pupils blown wide. "Your ex was a fucking idiot for making you feel ashamed of this. You're the hottest thing I've seen in ages with your mouth full of my cock."

Caitlin's pussy throbbed at Jas's words. She bent her head back to fully meet her eyes and took her a little deeper still. Her clit begged to be touched, her cunt to be filled, and the thought that Jas would do that to her soon nearly had her coming on the spot. She pulled back, then moved forward again, taking Jas even deeper, the head of her cock almost touching the back of her mouth. Okay, that was far enough; she had no desire to play around with deep-throating.

She repeated the pull back and moved in again, using Jas's cock to fuck her mouth. She could smell Jas now, her scent musky and sweet, filling her nostrils. Her own pussy lips were so swollen, she had to shift position to ease the discomfort.

Jas clenched her fingers on the back of Caitlin's head. "Oh, yeah. You're so good at this."

Caitlin groaned deep in the back of her throat and worked harder, her tongue diving at all angles around the now very warm silicone dildo. She clenched Jas's thighs tightly; if nothing else, it stopped her from shoving a hand in her own underwear and rubbing herself to what she was sure would be a huge orgasm. She looked up at Jas once more, thrilled to see the pleasure playing out across her features.

The woman's eyes were half-lidded, and her breathing quickened. "You keep doing that as long as you want. But I'm ready to fuck you whenever you like."

Caitlin eased Jas's cock out of her mouth. "Now. Please. I can't wait." Everything in her wanted to be filled. She didn't care how desperate she sounded.

Jas grinned and held out her hand.

She got to her feet; her knees screamed, and she stumbled a little as she stepped back half a pace.

"You okay?" Jas was there, holding her elbow.

"Fine. Not used to being on my knees so much."

Jas chuckled. "Well, you might need to. You're so fucking good at that."

The compliment made her smile. "Thanks. It was amazing. Everything I thought it would be."

The kiss from Jas was tender then. When they broke apart, Jas wasted no time in steering Caitlin over to the bench nearby.

At the sight of the padded leather, Caitlin's cunt throbbed. She'd never wanted to be fucked so badly.

Jas turned to her. "You're going to be pretty exposed doing it this way. I'm totally up for it, but just wanted you to know you can stop things anytime you like, okay?"

She still couldn't believe her luck in finding Jas tonight. Of all the women to make this fantasy come true, this caring and thoughtful woman was perfect. And hot too—maybe skinnier than Caitlin usually went for, but Jas had a deceptive strength that was enticing. "Thanks for saying that, but trust me, I definitely want this. Exactly how I said."

With a nod, Jas brushed her fingers down over Caitlin's breast, eliciting a soft moan Caitlin couldn't have held back even if she wanted to. "Then I'm going to get comfortable, and you need to get that underwear off and get ready to work."

Once again, the power of Jas's words robbed Caitlin of breath. She did as she was told, as fast as she could. Her G-string hit the floor somewhere near the wall; if she never found it again, she didn't care.

Jas lay down on the bench and shuffled to get comfy. Her cock jutted up from her open trousers. A wicked smile crossed her lips as she patted her thighs. "Sit. Now."

Her legs trembled as Caitlin took the final step to the bench. She had to hike her skirt up to step over Jas's body, and cool air brushed over her wet pussy as she did so. Anyone in the room, if they looked close enough, would be able to see her open and wet. She shivered; it felt deliciously dirty—and she felt absolutely no shame about it.

Jas gripped Caitlin's hips and tugged her down to her waiting cock. When the dildo nudged at her entrance, already slip-sliding through her copious wetness, Caitlin dipped her head to catch Jas's eyes. "Yes," she hissed, unashamedly.

That elicited a groan. Without hesitation, Jas thrust her hips up and buried the dildo deep inside Caitlin.

It hurt a little, and she cried out, but in the next moment, the minimal pain was overwhelmed by the pleasure of being filled. Of being filled by Jas's cock. "Oh fuck, yes." Her voice was strangled, her arousal so high that she could barely form the words.

"Jesus." Jas's voice was equally strained. "You are so wet for me."

"Uh-huh…" Caitlin's eyelids fluttered as pleasure swamped her.

Jas pulled out, not quite all the way, and held Caitlin's hips. "You want this so bad, don't you? Come on, take it. Fuck my cock." Her gaze bored into Caitlin's, the intensity almost overwhelming.

Oh God, did she want that. "Yes! *Yes!*"

Jas's groan was long as Caitlin thrust downwards, taking the whole length of Jas's cock inside her once more.

It was exquisite—everything she'd dreamed of and then some. Caitlin kept her gaze fixed on Jas's face as she pumped up and down. Her thighs complained, but she ignored them, instead leaning forward a little to grasp hold of Jas's shoulders.

Her gaze dropped to Caitlin's cleavage and she grinned. "Well, thanks for improving the view." She dipped into the front of Caitlin's top with one hand, keeping the other tight on Caitlin's hip. Without hesitating, Jas pushed Caitlin's bra cup to one side and squeezed her breast, rolling the hard nipple between her fingers. "You're so fucking sexy riding me like this." Her voice was a combination of rasp and grunt.

Everything coalesced inside Caitlin. The feel of Jas inside her. The rough treatment on her breast. The scorching look of desire on Jas's face. This wasn't just about what Caitlin wanted; it was obvious Jas gained a huge amount of pleasure from it too, and that only increased Caitlin's enjoyment of the moment.

Bracing herself against Jas's shoulders, she thrust faster up and down on the cock. She'd probably be sore in the morning, but right now she wanted all of it, as hard as she could get it.

They both made sounds Caitlin couldn't name as she rode those seven inches. Each thrust spiralled Caitlin deeper into a place she'd never visited, a kind of pleasure she'd only imagined. Her mind spun with it, her senses disorientated. She arched her head back as her pleasure climbed, and her eyes, momentarily open, locked gazes with a woman sitting at the centre table. They watched her, watched as Jas's cock plunged ever deeper into Caitlin's cunt.

The thrill of being someone's voyeuristic pleasure was almost as good as the fucking itself.

"I'm going to come." Jas's voice was hard with her arousal. "I'm going to—" She went deep, her hands digging so hard into Caitlin's flesh, both hip and breast; there'd be bruises in the morning. "Christ! Yes!" Jas kept herself pressed tight against Caitlin, her cock buried as deep as it could go, as she shuddered beneath her.

Knowing she'd done that to Jas, had made her feel that good, was one of the most powerful experiences Caitlin had had. She wanted to hold Jas, kiss her and feel her warmth. But she was also so close to coming herself. She needed that more than anything else right now. "Can you...?" She nodded with her head in the direction of her pussy.

Jas immediately removed her hand from inside the front of Caitlin's dress and released the pressure of her hips a little. "Want me to come out?"

"No! Stay, please. Just touch me. I want to come on your cock."

"Oh, holy fuck, yes!" Jas stared up at her, her lips parted, her breathing frantic again. She licked her thumb, and without hesitation, pressed it against Caitlin's clit.

Caitlin bucked. "Yes!"

"Jesus, you're so hard." Jas's eyes were heavy-lidded, her face set in a mask of concentration as she slicked her thumb over Caitlin's clit.

Caitlin was almost delirious with pleasure. The firm touch of Jas's thumb there made her cry out loud. A few strokes would finish her off—she knew that—but even though she was desperate to spin into that abyss, she wanted to make it last; it all still felt that good. Jas's cock, which had seemed so big at first sight, now barely stretched her. But the sensations it gave against the walls of her cunt were the perfect counterpoint to the incredible waves of pleasure Jas created by strumming her thumb over her clit.

Alternating between hard and soft strokes, long ones and quick little flicks, Jas held Caitlin's hip with her other hand, bracing her so that she had room to manoeuvre. "You look so fucking hot." Jas's voice was husky.

Caitlin *felt* hot, felt as if she was finally the sexual person she'd always wanted to be. She'd never have believed she'd find that with a stranger in the darkened room of a sex club, but the method didn't matter. It was the end result that was important, and her sense of fulfilment was almost as exciting as the arousal flooding her veins.

She couldn't hold it back any longer. Her need to come was overwhelming. She leaned farther into Jas's touch, which changed the angle of the dildo, and her world tilted. It was sublime even as it was torture. The pleasure was so intense, her heart rate increased to a frantic pace. Just two more firm strokes of Jas's thumb sent the wave slamming into her.

Everything inside her cunt tightened around Jas's cock, and Caitlin bucked against her as her orgasm consumed her. She let out a wrenching groan and collapsed forward, her limbs turning to jelly. Jas caught her up in her strong arms and urged her to lie down on her chest, wrapping her arms around Caitlin to hold her tight against her.

They clutched each other, breathing hotly into each other's ears. It felt so good, Caitlin didn't want to let go.

It took a couple of minutes, but Caitlin finally managed to breathe fully again, rather than the short, choppy gasps she was only capable of in the midst of her orgasm. She winced, aware of how tight Jas felt inside her. "Hm, I think you'd better come out now."

Jas relaxed her hold on Caitlin and smiled up at her. "Do what you need to."

Slowly but steadily, Caitlin eased back off the dildo until it popped free. She sat back on Jas's thighs, still too wobbly to stand. "Is this okay?"

"More than okay." Jay slid her hands along Caitlin's thighs to her waist. "Stay there as long as you need."

Caitlin smiled then shook her head. She ached in so many places and couldn't care less about any of them. "Oh my God, I don't think I'll be able to walk for a week!"

Jas laughed. "You gave me quite the workout. I'm pretty sure I'm going to be feeling that for a few days too."

Pride filled Caitlin. On top of that, the sense of release she'd felt throughout their encounter still coursed through her body. She'd never felt so free. Or satisfied. She smiled down at Jas, then raised her hands and ran them through her hair, shaking it out. Across the room, the woman who'd been watching her earlier gave her a big grin, and Caitlin laughed out loud.

"What?" Jas tried to look over her shoulder, then grinned. "Oh, you have a fan, huh?"

Caitlin smirked, then dared to see if her legs could hold her up. They weren't one hundred per cent happy with the idea, but she managed to stand.

Jas swung herself round to a sitting position, and Caitlin gingerly sat on the bench beside her. She watched as Jas stripped the condom off her cock and wrapped it in a tissue.

"I'll get rid of that in a minute." Jas shoved the package into her pocket. She tucked the dildo back into her trousers and zipped up, then blew out a long breath. "That was incredible. Thank you."

"Oh my God, no, thank *you*!" Caitlin shook her head. "You have no idea how long I've wanted to do that, and you made it perfect for me."

"I'm really glad about that. But trust me, I got a huge amount out of that too." Jas smiled.

"Is this…? Do you…?" Caitlin swallowed. She had so many questions, but did she have any right to ask? So they'd fucked—spectacularly. It didn't mean they had to have anything more to do with each other.

"It's okay, ask me." Jas leaned in a little so that their shoulders were touching.

"Do you come here a lot? And is this what you do when you're here? It's okay if you don't want to answer."

Jas's smile was so lovely, it made weirdly wonderful butterflies go crazy in Caitlin's stomach. "Are you interested in a repeat?"

Before Caitlin could think about how she'd want to answer that, Jas continued.

"Yeah, I do come here fairly regularly. And, yes, the kind of thing we just shared is usually what I do. I've been in and out of relationships the last couple of years, and right now I'm happy to be single and just have this place as an outlet now and then."

"And that's enough? I mean, I'm asking because I seem to have had a bad run of relationships, if you can even call them that, with women I really don't connect with. Maybe coming here on the regular could be the solution, for now." It was certainly tempting. Hot sex, just how she liked it, and no need to worry about all the emotional entanglements.

"It works for me." Jas looked around. "I do see a lot of the same faces in here, so it seems it must work for others too. Not sure what their reasons are, but I know for me, that's the beauty of this place. You can get from it just what you need, no questions asked. I don't see it as a long-term thing for me, but, yeah, right now it's perfect."

"Hm." Caitlin also looked around, noting all the different couplings happening in the room. There were so many possibilities she could explore, all with no strings attached.

"Okay, I'm going to go get cleaned up." Jas stood up.

"Good idea. Can you show me to the toilets?"

"Sure. And they're full-on bathrooms, by the way. Showers and everything."

"You're kidding!"

Jas grinned. "Nope. Single-occupancy only, though, so don't get any ideas."

"Damn." Caitlin laughed. Then she remembered her discarded G-string and began hunting for it.

"I think it ended up somewhere there." Jas pointed to an area of wall nearby.

Caitlin stepped forward, her gaze scanning the ground. There! She scooped up the G-string and scrunched it into a ball. Yeah, maybe she'd be going home without underwear. Lesson learned for next time: bring a spare pair.

Jas held out her hand. "Come on, I'll walk you over there."

Caitlin took Jas's warm hand in hers and sighed happily. "Thanks for being here tonight. I'm so glad it was you I did this with."

Jas squeezed her hand. "Me too."

They reached the bathrooms, and each stood before one of the doors to the cubicles.

"If I don't see you when I leave," Jas said, "have a nice rest of your evening, okay?"

"I will. I might stay and watch some things for a while."

"That's always a good way to spend an evening."

They stared at each other for a moment, gazes locked.

"Well, bye, then." Caitlin wanted to say more, to ask more, but they'd had their fun, and that was that, wasn't it?

Jas shuffled her feet. "You know, I was planning on visiting again next Saturday." She looked down at her feet, then back up again. "If you're around, maybe we could…?"

Caitlin's breath caught, and her body thrummed once more. "Oh yeah, I think we could."

Jas's lifted her chin. "Good to know."

Nodding, Caitlin pushed the cubicle door open. "Until next week, then." Without waiting for an answer, she closed the door, her smile so wide it made her cheeks ache.

CHAPTER 5

MANDY

THE TRAIN PULLED IN TO Brighton station at a little before 1 p.m., exactly as scheduled, and Mandy stood as it slowed its approach to the platform. After pulling her overnight bag down from the rack above her head, she joined the other passengers already heading for the door. Her stomach clenched a little as she waited to exit the train, and she tamped it down in annoyance.

Come on. It's just a visit with a friend. That's all.

A part of her still didn't quite understand how they'd got to this point. This would be about the fifth time they'd seen each other since that first night Laura had appeared at the club. They'd ended that lunch on the Sunday swapping phone numbers—but just to keep in touch, they'd both said.

A few weeks later, after they'd begun to swap messages on WhatsApp on a fairly regular basis, Laura had suggested another lunch. She had travelled up for the weekend and spent Saturday lunchtime with Mandy but hadn't come to the club on either the Friday or Saturday evenings. Mandy had tried hard not to read too much into that, nor into how easy she found it to be in Laura's company and to talk and laugh with her.

Their messages on WhatsApp morphed into occasional phone calls that lasted an hour, or two, which Mandy came to look forward to more than anything in her week.

And so now, here Mandy was in Brighton on a Thursday lunchtime in the middle of July with a hotel room booked at the Grand and a return ticket for Friday tucked in her handbag. Coming to Laura this time had made sense: the Georgia O'Keeffe exhibition wasn't touring to Manchester for another six months; of course it was the best plan to see it earlier here in Brighton. And it seemed only fair, given that Laura had now twice made the long trip to Manchester.

As Mandy exited the train and stepped onto the platform, she almost tutted out loud. *Yes, those are all the rational reasons why you're here, but they're not the real reason, are they?*

She brushed the thought aside and walked down the platform, where she could see Laura waiting for her.

"Hey, you made it!" Laura stepped forward and took Mandy's bag, waving off her protests. "It's great to see you."

"And you."

"How was the journey?"

"Long but fine. It's actually quite nice to have to change trains a couple of times, isn't it? Get some air, stretch the legs."

Laura smiled. "It is." She gazed at Mandy for a moment, then blinked. "So, um, hungry? I booked a table, but if you'd rather wait, we can—"

"Actually, I'm starving!" Mandy grinned when Laura burst out laughing.

"Well, all right then, let's get you fed. Come on. By some miracle, I managed to park only a couple of streets away."

They walked out into the sunshine, and Mandy lifted her face up, delighting in the swirl of seagulls above her head, the blue sky a perfect backdrop for the birds' white and grey bodies.

"Feel good?" Laura asked softly.

Mandy met her warm look. "Yes. Perfect."

Laura nodded, then motioned for Mandy to head to a pedestrian crossing a few yards away. "Over there and round the corner."

They walked in comfortable silence until they were away from the noise and bustle around the station.

"It's great that you're here," Laura said as they turned into a quieter street. "And I'm so looking forward to seeing the exhibition."

"Yes! As soon as they announced this one, I knew I would have to see it somehow. It's—it's lovely to share it with someone rather than go on my own."

Laura's warm smile returned, and she nodded. "It really is."

Mandy tried hard to ignore the flutter in her stomach.

A minute later, Laura gestured across the street. "So, here we are. Not the classiest chariot for you, milady, but it'll get us there." She pointed to the small van emblazoned with her landscaping company's logo.

Mandy chuckled. "It's got four wheels and an engine; it's good enough for me."

Laura unlocked the doors, placed Mandy's bag carefully in the back on a clean tarpaulin that presumably covered equipment and supplies, then closed Mandy's door for her once she was settled in the passenger seat. The chivalry felt natural, not staged, and it warmed Mandy's heart. *She's an old-fashioned woman. I like it.*

They drove out of the city and along the coast, windows open to let the warm breeze flow between them, chatting about their respective weeks and the gorgeous scenery around them.

About fifteen minutes later, Laura slowed the van and pulled them into a pub car park, then turned off the engine. "Here we are."

"Great. Looks lovely."

They exited the van.

"Yeah, it's been a favourite for a couple of years," Laura said. "After Kelly died, I tried to find new places that weren't swamped with memories, you know?"

Mandy nodded, and followed Laura to the pub entrance. "I understand."

They were seated at a small table in the pub's dining area and soon ordered their food from the menu filled with pub classics.

"God, I can't remember the last time I ate proper pub food." Mandy grinned over her glass of water.

"We can still go somewhere fancier, if that's more your thing?"

"God, no!" Mandy squeezed Laura's hand without thinking, then blinked when she realised what she'd done and pulled her hand back. "This is lovely."

Laura flicked a glance to where their hands had been joined, then smiled. "Good." She took a sip of her drink. "So, how has business been?"

"Very good. I'm actually considering opening longer on Saturday nights. I've had quite a lot of people mention on their way out that they'd prefer it."

"Hm, more work for you though, right?"

Mandy shrugged. "I don't mind. And maybe I could hire another person to help out, ease the workload. It's been on my mind."

"Would that mean you might get some Saturdays off in the future?"

"Perhaps." Mandy tilted her head, noting the nervous way Laura tapped her fingers on her beer mat.

"I was, er, just wondering because, well, it'd be great to be able to visit some more at weekends. You know, go out to dinner, maybe?"

Mandy's stomach swirled pleasantly at the thought. *Calm down, she just means friendship. Doesn't she?* "Yes, that would be lovely."

"Are you seeing anyone?" Laura's question came quickly, seeming to surprise even herself.

Mandy laughed, but it was wobbly. "No. Why?"

"Well, um, I'm just assuming that you would have more free time to see me, but, obviously, if there is someone special in the picture, I wouldn't want to impose or get in the way or…" Laura visibly swallowed and quickly reached for her drink once more.

See, she just wants friendship. "No," Mandy said quietly. "There's no one." *Although I wish there was.* There, she'd admitted it. And she was pretty sure she knew who she wanted that someone to be. "If only," she muttered.

"What did you say?" Laura leaned forward, her gaze intent.

Mandy's mouth went dry. *Fuck, she wasn't supposed to hear that!* "Um, nothing."

Laura licked her lips, made to say something, then sat back. "Okay." She smiled, but it wasn't anywhere near her best. "I must be hearing things. Getting old." She winked.

Mandy's laugh was hollow to her own ears.

Their food arrived a couple of minutes later, much to Mandy's relief, as it steered their conversation away to easier, less heart-pounding subjects. Within minutes, they'd both relaxed again and were back on even ground.

The meal was wonderful, as was the conversation they shared around it, and they were both stuffed when they finished.

"Shit, I'm not sure I'll be able to spend two hours on my feet at an exhibition now." Mandy chuckled ruefully. "I'll maybe manage a slow waddle. Is that all right?"

Laura laughed and patted her own middle. "We'll waddle together, don't worry."

It's so easy to be with her. Mandy basked in it, smiling as Laura joked with their waitress when it came time to pay. Comfortable, but not boring. Easy, and fun, and…nice. She squirmed inside. *Nice* wasn't even close to describing it.

"Ready to go?" Laura looked across the table at her.

"Yes. Definitely." Mandy stood, her mind still churning over her thoughts. It had been a long time since she'd built a new friendship. It was a little nerve-wracking getting to know someone new, but she also knew she had to be honest with herself and acknowledge there was something underlying it all that made her more nervous: her growing attraction to Laura.

But it really didn't seem her attraction was reciprocated. Or was it?

Jesus, I'm too old to get my heart broken all over again.

Again, Mandy did what she'd done over the last few weeks whenever this knowledge intruded on her thoughts—she pushed it away, locked it up tight in a little corner somewhere in the hopes that it could be forgotten.

They drove back into the city and left the van in a car park a few minutes' walk away from the Royal Pavilion, where the exhibition was being held. After a slow stroll through the streets, they arrived at their allotted entry time and Laura handed over their tickets to be scanned.

It was busy inside but not uncomfortable, and they eagerly walked into the start of the exhibition.

"Oh, wow!" Mandy stopped and stared at the paintings on the walls around her. "Seeing so many of her pieces all at once is fantastic."

"Isn't it?" Laura beamed at her. "I'm so glad we're doing this."

The warmth in her gaze made all sorts of delicious things happen to Mandy's insides but she inwardly battened down her defences even as she nodded and smiled at Laura. So what if Laura wasn't interested in her in any other way than as a friend? This was great, sharing special things like this together. It was enough. More than enough.

Wasn't it?

"Oh, hi, Laura. Come on in."

Nina closed the shutter in the door, then opened the door itself. "Nice to see you again," she said as she motioned Laura into the hallway of the club.

"Thanks, you too. I know I'm a little early, but the walk over here didn't take as long as I thought it would." Laura followed Nina into the office.

"No worries. You can sit here until she's done. She's just walking the rooms before she goes." Nina smiled. "She likes to do that."

"I know." Laura also knew Mandy would have already packed her bag to be ready when Laura arrived because she hated to keep anyone waiting. And she knew Mandy would probably be wearing dressy trousers and a gorgeous shirt because that was her go-to outfit for an evening here at the club.

Laura knew so much about Mandy and her life. Except for one thing: did Mandy feel this growing...connection between them, or was it just Laura?

"You okay?" Nina asked.

"What?" Laura eased the frown from her face. "Yes, fine. Thanks."

Laura had been distracted ever since Mandy's visit to Brighton a couple of weeks back. It had been such a great visit, and they'd spent so much time together. And it hadn't been until they'd been saying goodbye at the station after brunch together on Friday morning that Laura had realised how much she would miss Mandy being close by.

And then it had hit her, like a cartoon sledgehammer, and she'd driven home in a complete daze to spend the afternoon staring into space, going over all the memories of their time together—how being with Mandy made her feel so good. How every time Mandy smiled, and those creases deepened at the corners of her eyes, Laura wanted to rub her thumbs over them, then down over her cheeks to her lips. How she wanted to replace her thumbs with her own lips, kiss that full mouth, and learn what Mandy tasted like...

She shook her head as she became aware that Nina was speaking again.

"...really looking forward to tonight."

"I'm sorry, what?"

"Are you sure you're okay?" Nina tilted her head, her dark hair falling across one shoulder. "I mean, tell me if it's none of my business, but you don't seem really with it tonight."

Laura rubbed her hands over her face and let out a breath. "Yeah, sorry. Got some things on my mind. What were you saying about tonight?"

"I was telling you how Mandy was really looking forward to it. And that I'm happy to be able to give her a bit of the night off."

"Yeah, I really appreciate that. It's great to be able to take her out on a Saturday night."

"Oh yeah, must be really hard trying to date someone who works every weekend."

"We're not dating!" Laura said quickly, heat rising to her cheeks.

Nina blinked a couple of times. "You're not?"

"No. Nope. Just friends."

"Really? At the risk of sounding cheeky, from my side it really doesn't look like you're not dating."

"Has Mandy said anything?" Laura asked the question before she could second-guess herself.

Nina's smile was a little teasing. "Not so much said. More like..." She twirled her hands in the air. "More like she gets all jumpy and, you know, *flustered* every time you two have something arranged. At first, I thought it was just because she can't stand leaving this place for even a minute, but lately I'm not so sure."

I shouldn't be having this conversation with Mandy's assistant. But fuck it. "Do you think she's open to dating? Hypothetically speaking, of course."

"Asking for a friend?" Nina smirked, then her expression turned serious. "Maybe." She fiddled with the papers piled on the desk. "I know she lost someone a couple of years back. Someone she cared about. I overheard her talking to Dee once about it. About how she wasn't sure she had it in her to fall for anyone again."

"I can relate." Laura sighed. Maybe this was stupid, thinking she and Mandy could become something—even if she now thought that perhaps, maybe, Mandy did reciprocate some or all of the attraction Laura felt.

"I do know one thing, though," Nina said, her tone gentle. "And I'm not an expert or anything, but you learn a lot about how to read people when you work somewhere like this."

Laura nodded, waiting for her to go on.

"She lights up every time your name is mentioned." Nina paused and smiled. "Every time."

Laura took a moment to digest those words, but before she could respond a door opened and closed in the hallway behind her. She turned just as Mandy strode into the office.

"Oh! You're here." Mandy smiled, her gorgeous blue eyes full of warmth. "I'm so excited about sneaking off early." She laughed. "I feel like I'm playing hooky from school."

Laura smiled, drinking in the sight of Mandy, her outfit just as stunning as Laura had expected. "Am I a bad influence?"

Mandy threw her a dazzling smile. "The *best* influence."

Over Mandy's shoulder, Nina nodded slowly at Laura, her smile knowing and smug.

"So, I'll be back at the end of the night to count the cash ready for banking." Mandy was all business again.

"You sure?" Nina stepped forward. "Why don't you just take the whole night off, rather than interrupting your evening out. We can just bag it all and leave it in the safe for you."

Mandy paused as she picked up her handbag. "I—while I appreciate the offer, I don't think that's necessary. It's easy enough for me to come back here on my way home."

Laura glanced between the two of them, seeing Nina's blatant attempt to give her boss a whole night off being stonewalled by Mandy's need to keep everything in order here at the club. On the one hand she could understand. On the other, she would have loved it if Mandy would just say to heck with it, and not give them a time limit on their evening.

Nina opened her mouth then closed it again. She spread her arms wide. "Then, off you go. Have a nice time, and I'll see you later."

"Thanks." Mandy turned to Laura. "Ready?"

"Absolutely." Laura threw Nina a wave.

The dark-haired woman shrugged and mouthed, *I tried. Sorry.*

Laura nodded, then turned her full attention to Mandy, who was now striding to the front door.

CHAPTER 6

JODY

"Good morning."

Jody looked up at the sound of her boss's voice and forced a smile. Suzanne was a nice woman, but Jody would bet every penny she owned she knew exactly what was on Suzanne's mind and therefore what she was about to say.

I knew I should have just booked the day off. But the idea of bumming around at home doing fuck all on this particular day had seemed worse than being here.

Jody's body tensed. "Hey."

Suzanne, her glossy blonde hair held back in its usual ponytail, smiled and handed over a bunch of manifest forms. "I know it's gone ten, but I need these processed by noon. Any chance you can do that?"

Jody blinked. Okay, so that wasn't what she'd expected Suzanne to say. At all. "Um, sure. I mean, only if you're happy for me to be a bit late on the September schedule updates."

"Totally. These take precedent."

Jody grabbed the forms and laid them down on her desk.

"Thanks, Jody. You're a star." Suzanne threw her another smile then strode away, leaving the sweet scent of her expensive perfume in her wake.

Jody breathed it in, then sat back. Her boss had surprised her, and in a good way. *Respect.*

A text message chimed on her phone. Sheila. Of course.

Hi, Jody. I know today is an important milestone. I'm here if you need to talk. Sheila.

Jody sucked in a breath. Her therapist somehow always seemed to know just when Jody needed a little boost. She honestly didn't know how she would have got through the last few months without her. Despite the heavy significance of today, she was miles better than she had been six months previously, and Sheila had definitely helped to keep her afloat no matter what angry and emotional outbursts Jody had thrown at her.

Thanks. Doing okay. See you Thursday.

Message sent, she reached for her coffee mug but realised it was empty. Oh yeah, she'd already finished her first cup of the day a while ago. Well, then, a second one was in order, especially as she would now be even busier for the morning than she'd anticipated.

The coffee machine, one of those fancy Nespresso things, stood on top of a small, waist-high cupboard in the corner of the room. Jody knew the machines weren't brilliant for the environment, but given how easy they made making a cup of coffee, especially for someone with one arm, she wasn't going to complain. She opened the chamber where the pod would be inserted, then took a fresh one out of the jar Suzanne always kept stocked up. A couple of moves later and her coffee streamed into her mug. A splash of milk and she was all set.

Maybe, in a couple of months, when she'd saved up a bit more, she could treat herself to one of these machines. The old-fashioned filter pot at home wasn't the easiest to work with.

Sure, she'd gradually got the hang of it in the twelve months since the accident, but…

Just as she got back to her desk, the phone rang. Kris's name came up in the caller display.

"Hey!" Jody sat down as she answered and rotated her chair back into position at her desk to maintain her centre of gravity.

The sound of a truck starting up came down the line. "Hey! We just finished unloading on the first job, and I've got a few mins spare, so thought I'd give you a call." Kris's smooth voice went muffled as she said something to a colleague, and then she was back. "Sorry, Dave's being a wanker."

"As usual." Jody smiled, knowing full well Kris got on just fine with her colleague; he was like a big brother to her.

"I know, right? So, anyway, I was thinking we should hit Dazzle tomorrow night, and I'm not taking no for an answer."

Jody smiled. Of course Kris would come up with a plan to take her mind off the anniversary. And of course she wouldn't allow Jody to refuse. "Bossy."

"Whatever. I'll pick you up. What time works for you?"

Dazzle wasn't really where Jody wanted to go. It was a tacky night out at the best of times, especially in the heat of mid-August with everyone wearing their skimpiest outfits. Tacky wasn't what she needed. In fact, she knew just what she did need, or at least she thought she did. But she couldn't get into that on the phone with Kris, and especially not at work.

"I'm definitely up for going out. But I've got another idea. Something a bit…different. Call me later, and I'll tell you all about it, okay?"

"Well, you're being mysterious. I like it." Kris laughed. "All right. And remind me when I call you that I need to tell you what just happened."

"Something juicy?"

"No, just fucking hilarious. It involves a parrot that can swear in three different languages and a bunch of Jehovah's Witnesses who *definitely* chose the wrong time to welcome the newcomers to the neighbourhood." Kris snorted with laughter, and Jody could hear Dave joining in in the background.

She smiled. "Okay, that totally sounds like a story I need to hear. Honestly, you have way too much fun moving people in and out of houses. I never would have realised."

"I know, I fucking love it! Right, laters."

"Cool."

They hung up, and Jody sat for a moment. Not only had Kris, yet again, put a big smile on her face, she'd also made sure Jody was okay on this particular day without actually asking outright. She really was the best friend anyone could ask for.

And tomorrow, I'm going to ask her to do something that might be really weird, even for two people who've been as good friends as we have.

She glanced around, checking to make sure Suzanne was definitely back in her own office. Then she opened up the browser on her phone and looked for about the hundredth time at the advert she'd found on the website of a women-only sex shop. The advert had spoken of something that could go a long way to helping her. The trouble was, she didn't fancy going on her own.

Would Kris be up for it? Or would she just laugh Jody out of the room?

Jody huffed out a breath. Only one way to find out.

That night after work, Jody slouched on the sofa, flicking through Netflix for some inspiration for what to binge watch next. Nothing grabbed her, so she put the remote back on the coffee table and stood. It had been hard to focus on anything tonight, not surprisingly. Although, of course, Kris's quick call just after Jody got home from work had helped. Kris always knew just what type of story Jody needed to hear about some of the weird people Kris met in her work as a van driver, especially when Jody was in need of distraction. And the parrot story had definitely been worth hearing.

But now, at a little past nine-thirty, Jody didn't know what she needed to calm her mind before sleep. She needed something to relax her, but beer wouldn't do it. Music, maybe. She paced the living room. Nah, not that. Then she stopped her pacing and smiled as a thought took hold.

Yeah, okay. Maybe *that* would work.

Her sexual appetite had been non-existent in the first eight or nine months following the accident, but lately glimmers of it had started to reappear, spurred on by re-reading some old erotica favourites from her meagre collection. When she'd eventually worked up the courage to touch herself about a month ago, trying to figure out what could work for her now, she hadn't come, but she also hadn't felt nothing.

What a relief that had been. Changing the habit of a lifetime because it was physically impossible to do anything else was frustrating, yet at the same time she'd been pleasantly surprised at how determined she was to overcome that obstacle. Sex had always played an important part in her life and she refused to let her accident stop her from being a sexual person.

At least with herself. She'd see about how it might feel with someone else if she managed to get to that club tomorrow night.

But for now, maybe some self-care would be in order. She was mildly turned on just at the thought and hurried to the bedroom to undress before she lost the impetus.

She closed the window—none of her neighbours needed to hear any sounds she might make, thank you very much—switched off the lamp, then slipped under the sheet. It had been a hot day, and the bedroom was little stifling with the window shut, but it would have to do. She yanked the sheet down off her body before she sweated too much. Hm, that actually felt good, being exposed to the air, her legs wide open. *Fuck, yeah, that feels amazing.*

With her eyes closed she let her mind wander to her favourite fantasy woman: long hair spilling over naked shoulders, big breasts, and long legs. Oh yeah, fantasy woman was definitely delivering tonight; Jody was already pretty wet at the thought of running her hands—

She sighed as the familiar pain hit, but then pushed past it. She'd use her tongue in her fantasy instead; there wasn't anything wrong with the way *that* worked. The picture she quickly conjured up had her squirming, imagining the woman begging Jody to make her come, telling her how desperate she was to come in Jody's mouth.

Jody's breathing quickened and turned a little ragged as her imaginary lover cocooned Jody's head between her hot thighs, the juice from her cunt running down over Jody's chin.

With a groan, she knew she was ready to touch herself now, to see what she could make happen. She'd always been someone who liked to use both hands, one to slip a finger inside while the other worked her clit. Obviously, that wasn't possible now; she could have either sensation, not both. But last weekend, she'd used a slightly different angle, coming at her clit more from the side than directly over the top.

Her fingers were thoroughly soaked within seconds of running them over her cunt, and they slipped easily over her clit when she dragged them back. *Oh yeah. Fuck, that's pretty good.* She twisted her wrist a little, searching for that spot that had nearly…done the…trick…last week—

The moan that left her throat in the next moment would definitely have disturbed the neighbours if that window had stayed open. *Jesus, that was…*

"Fuck!" she said aloud as the tips of her fingers rubbed quickly across a small area on the right side of her clit, just under the hood, generating an explosive level of arousal within seconds. Her phantom arm ached to join in, but she worked hard to focus all her attention on the fingers of her right hand, working away at that spot, rubbing harder now, harder, harder…

The orgasm slammed into her so quickly, so fiercely that any cry of ecstasy she might have made stuck in her throat. Her hips jacked upwards, and her eyes squeezed shut as her body convulsed with wave after wave of pleasure of the kind she hadn't felt in such a long time. Finally stilling her fingers, she slumped back to the bed as a whoosh of a breath left her lungs. Her breathing was heavy in the darkness.

A smile that made her cheeks ache spread across her lips. Well, *that* had certainly blown a lot of her ghosts away. Maybe she *was* ready for tomorrow night.

"So, how's life in the glamorous world of shipping?" Kris asked as she followed Jody into the tiny kitchen of her flat.

"Probably about as exciting as the glamorous world of removals." Jody pointed at Kris. "And don't be dissing my work. You know what it's like, remember?"

"Ha-ha! Yeah, true." Kris shrugged. "It wasn't the worst place to work. It was fun when we worked the floor together."

"Exactly!"

"But I gotta say, I do prefer the job I've got now."

"Fair enough." Jody pulled a Becks out of the fridge for herself and placed it on the counter, then reached back into the fridge for an alcohol-free IPA, one from Kris's favourite brand. She used the bottle-opener screwed to the wall next to the fridge to pop the caps and handed the IPA to Kris.

Kris took it with a big smile on her face. "Aw, you remembered!" Her blue eyes sparkled.

"Of course. I'm the nice one, remember?" Jody picked up her own beer and motioned to the kitchen door.

"You're so fucking funny."

They laughed and walked through to the living room. After sitting on the small sofa, they tapped bottles and took a long drink.

"Very nice." Kris admired the bottle in her hand.

"Only the best for you, mate."

Kris rolled her eyes, and Jody laughed.

"So, how's things now with Caitlin?"

Kris blinked. "Um, fine. It's like it never happened, which is great. We just have a laugh now. My guess is she's seeing someone coz she seems really happy. Why?"

"I suppose I still don't get why you didn't go for it. She sounded like exactly your type." It had baffled Jody, in fact. This Caitlin was the sort of woman Kris would normally climb over hot coals to be with. Or, at least, would have done in the past.

Something had changed in Kris in the last few months. They'd never talked about it, mainly because Jody had been wrapped up in her own head in the aftermath of last year. *Shit, I've been a crap friend. She's been here for me through all of this, and I've never asked her what's going on with her.*

Kris shrugged and took another gulp of beer.

"You okay?" Jody tried to catch Kris's eye. "I know you're the silent type, so it's cool if you don't want to talk but—"

"I'm good." Kris's words were clipped. A clear sign to end that line of discussion.

"So, broken any other hearts recently?" Jody grinned, hoping to lift her friend out of her slump.

"Shut up." Kris rolled her eyes, her lips twitching as if she was holding back a smile.

"What? Come on, all the years we've been hanging out together, all the places we've been, you're the one with the biggest trail of devastated women behind you."

Kris belly-laughed. "*Riiiight.* You're about two behind me, max. You give them those dark-brown puppy eyes, and they're queueing up. Sometimes it's like I'm invisible when I'm standing right next to you!"

"You're hilarious." Jody sipped her beer. "So, how's your mum?"

Kris shrugged. "She's okay. Loves that sofa we found for her, by the way. Won't shut up about it actually."

"And the dickhead?"

"Not a word from him. Your mate on the force paying him that unofficial visit definitely seems to have scared him off."

"Yeah, I'm not sure I'd want a surprise visit from Luke late at night. Built like a brick shithouse he is."

"Good." Kris's expression was grim, then softened. "And thanks. Again. What you did that night was above and beyond."

"Oh, come on; you'd have done the same. That's... I mean, that's us, isn't it? Always there for each other? You've done tons for me this last year that more than pays me back for helping get rid of that asshole from your mum's life." Jody swallowed. "If I haven't thanked you properly before, I'm doing it now. I don't know what I would have done without you since, you know, the accident."

Kris blushed and nudged Jody's hip. In doing so, she inadvertently brushed Jody's stump.

Jody couldn't help but flinch and regretted doing so as soon as she moved.

"Shit! Sorry. Did I catch a tender spot?" Kris's eyes were wide with concern.

Jody eased back a little on the sofa, heat infusing her cheeks. *Why do I still always overreact?* It had been a year since the freak accident with the warehouse lifting equipment left her looking like this. Surely that was long enough to be normal again, wasn't it?

Don't be so hard on yourself, the little voice inside Jody's head that was Sheila's told her. Her therapist would also tell her to have patience, and to certainly not use words like "normal" to describe anything and blah blah blah. "Nah, all good. It doesn't hurt. I just...I just can't seem to help being nervous about it still."

Kris's gaze dropped to the stump of Jody's left arm, the end of it visible from the sleeve of her T-shirt, and Jody swallowed hard. Anyone staring so directly at it, even Kris, made her stomach tighten.

"So really, how was yesterday?" Kris's voice was low and quiet. She met Jody's gaze. "You said no one said anything."

Jody shook her head. "Nope. Not even Suzanne."

"Well, that's good, right? I mean, you didn't want the anniversary to be anything big, so..."

"Yeah, it's good." Jody took another mouthful of beer. "It was on my mind more than I wanted, though. Like my brain didn't get the message that I wanted to treat it like any other day, even if everyone else did."

"Sorry."

"It is what it is. Maybe by the next anniversary it won't matter so much, and the one after that it'll be even less. But it pisses me off I probably won't ever forget the date as long as I work there." She lifted her left shoulder and felt her phantom fingers spreading in a "what can you do?" gesture.

"I get that." Kris made to say more, then closed her mouth.

"What?"

"Nothing." Kris ran a hand over her head, the slight rasp of the shaved hair against her fingers sounding loud between them. "So, what's this big secret plan you've cooked up for tonight?"

Grateful for the change of topic—and for Kris so pointedly ignoring that she was wearing a T-shirt for the first time since the accident—Jody twisted a little in her seat to be able to face her. "You have to promise not to get all judge-y, okay?"

Kris frowned. "Okay." She drew the word out. "But you know that's not like me, right?"

"I know, it's just..." Jody took another slug of beer. Jesus, why was this so hard to say? She and Kris had been friends for years and had shared so much of each other's lives—and so many nights out where they had picked up women, or helped each other to. This wouldn't be that much different.

Her face heated at the thought. Yeah, okay, maybe it was a *bit* different.

"Why are you blushing?" Kris stared at her.

"Shit." Jody ducked her head. Maybe it would be easier if she didn't actually look at Kris. "So, there's this club I've heard of. Women only. It's kind of…specialised."

"Huh?"

Jody huffed out a breath. "It's a sex club." She spoke quickly before Kris could cut her off. "And I really want to go. But I'm kind of nervous about going on my own, so would you…?"

Finally daring to look up, she met Kris's wide-eyed gaze.

"A sex club?" Kris blinked. "What does that even mean?"

"Remember how we read that magazine article once about how gay men had all those darkrooms, back before AIDS took hold?"

She nodded.

"Well, it's kind of like a darkroom for women. Actually, there's three rooms, apparently. All for, like, different tastes."

"You're not actually joking, are you?" Kris put her beer on the table and clasped her knees.

Quite suddenly, Jody noted how cool Kris looked tonight in her button-up Levi's and skintight, dark blue T-shirt. All of it looked like it was tailor-made for her skinny frame, and the snug T-shirt nicely showed off her pierced nipples. *She'll have the women in the club begging for her within minutes.* The thought filled her with sadness—it wasn't like she'd have the same success. But maybe she'd find one woman willing to look past the obvious.

"No, I'm not. Look, you know how I feel about dating and all that now. You know, since the accident."

Kris glared at her. "Yeah, and you know I think it's a load of bollocks."

"I don't want to argue tonight." Jody kept her voice calm.

"All right." Kris exhaled loudly. "So, let me guess, you think going to a darkroom is a pretty safe way for you to get your kicks without having to worry about what anyone might think of you only having one arm." The heat—and disapproval—in Kris's tone was unmistakable.

"Yep, that is exactly how I feel." Jody wasn't sure how the words got out; her teeth were clenched so tight. "It'll be really dark in there. No one will be able to see much." She sighed and used her thumb to flick at the peeling corner of her beer bottle. "I miss being with someone."

Kris looked at Jody for a moment, her entire body stilled. "You could be with anyone you wanted," she said quietly.

"Could I? Really? Did you see that girl at the pub garden last week? The one who nearly dropped her drink when my shirt arm came unpinned and flapped in the breeze?"

"I did, and, yes, her reaction was fucked-up. But most people haven't been like that."

"That isn't how I feel. I feel like everyone is always staring and can't see beyond the missing arm to the person behind it." Jody's words came out on a whisper. "And I want to go somewhere where I don't have to worry about that. Where everyone's there just for a quick, physical thing, no questions asked. I need to get this out of my system. I need to just *feel* other things, even if it's just for one night. I know you don't understand, or agree, but I need this. Please."

Kris slumped back and ran both hands over her head. "Okay," she mumbled. "I'm sorry. I just..." She blinked rapidly, then looked away, swallowing hard.

They sat in silence for a couple of minutes.

Jody knew Kris eventually would support her, even if she didn't agree with her. But would Kris come to the club with her and let Jody try this way of bringing something physical back into her life?

She finished her beer and carefully leaned forward to put the empty bottle on the table.

Kris stood up. "Right." She smiled, but it didn't quite reach her eyes. "How long is it gonna take us to get to this club?"

"*Soooo,*" Kris said after they took their drinks from the barwoman and strolled over to a long table in the centre of the room. "Here we are."

Jody didn't think she'd ever been so nervous in a women-only space. *Stupid.* Her nerves had been building through the car ride here, to the point where she'd nearly told Kris to turn the car around. She'd checked the sleeve of her shirt about fifty times as they drove, even though she knew the way she'd pinned it in place was totally secure.

Kris had said nothing when Jody pulled the shirt on just before they left the house. She'd probably guessed, quite rightly, that Jody's confidence had deserted her at the last minute.

Little steps. Just going to the club was big enough without having her stump on full display. She could have worn the prosthetic, but it was heavy, and the pretend hand on the end sometimes gave her the creeps. That was the last thing she needed when she was trying to build up her confidence.

Little steps. That's what Sheila had been teaching her. Little steps back to normality. Of course, her normality would be a new one, but lately she'd started to allow herself to believe her new normality might be an okay place to be. And that was massive progress compared to where she'd been six months ago.

Enough of that. You're here now. Even if you don't actually do anything, you can still enjoy yourself. She gazed across the room at a couple kissing deeply against the far wall. *Hell yeah.*

She and Kris each pulled out a stool and sat. Jody wobbled for a moment, adjusting her centre of gravity on the high stool to account for the lack of weight on her left side but shooed off Kris's offer to help with a quick look.

Kris rolled her eyes and smirked at Jody's need for independence, as usual not letting her get away with any bullshit.

Jody gave her the middle finger once she'd got herself balanced, and they smiled at each other.

Her friend sat on Jody's left as usual. They'd never spoken about it, Jody had never asked Kris to do it, but every time they'd been out—since Jody had felt comfortable being out and about again—Kris had always taken that side. *I guess she's making sure no one bumps me. Huh, funny—I never thought about how protective she's been all this time.* She smiled inwardly; she wouldn't embarrass them both by mentioning it.

She focused her attention back on the room. They were in something called the Green Room. They'd thought they'd start here for one drink, then maybe check out the action in the other rooms, just to see what was on offer.

"How you feeling?" Kris's eyes were shadowed in the dim room, but her voice gave away her concern.

She could lie, say it was all okay. But this was Kris. "Bricking it, actually." She waved her hand in the direction of the rest of the room. "I'm not sure I'm actually going to do anything here tonight. You know, other than watch."

"Yeah, okay." Kris looked away.

Jody took a mouthful of beer, then placed her bottle on the table and looked around. Directly across from them was a threesome; to their right, someone was being fucked over the back of a chair.

She glanced at Kris to gauge her reaction to what was on display. "Hot, huh?"

"Yeah." Kris's tone lacked conviction. She swept her gaze over Jody's shirt. "Sure you're not too hot in that?"

Jody tugged at the buttoned-up collar and grinned. "Only from the smoking hot scenes in front of me." It was a bluff; she was way too warm in the shirt, but there was no way she would take it off. They hadn't exactly interacted with anyone since arriving, but the dark colour of the shirt and the darkness of the room had certainly seemed to ensure that no one spotted what was wrong with her. She mentally tutted; she was better than she used to be, but negative and damaging language still popped into her brain. More stuff for Sheila to work with.

Kris gave her half a smile. "You know, no one would notice anything, if you took it off. It's way too dark in here."

Jody swallowed. "Not yet."

"Hey, I'm not pushing, okay?" Kris leaned in a little. "It's just… Well, you kind of wanted this place to be a test, right? So…"

"I know." Jody hated that her voice was so small. She cleared her throat. "Maybe later." She downed the rest of her beer.

"Want another one?" Kris was only halfway through her own beer.

"No, not yet."

"Okay." Kris gave her a penetrating look but said nothing else.

"So," Jody said after a beat, "the woman who took our money when we came in, what did she say about how to let someone know you're interested?"

Kris blinked a couple of times before answering. "Stand against a wall." She gestured to the long table where they sat. "This is a no-go zone. I mean, I guess you can check someone out from here, maybe make some eye contact. But nothing can actually happen while you're sat here."

"Yeah, right." Jody had known that, of course, but the nerves had scrambled the information.

"Why are you asking?" Kris's voice croaked. "You want to—?"

"No!" Jody realised she'd spoken louder than she intended. "No, I just forgot, and I don't want to get into something I'm not ready for just because I couldn't remember the bloody rules."

"Okay. Cool."

They sat in silence for a few moments.

Jody didn't know who Kris was watching, but she kept getting drawn to the threesome in front of them. She'd never had one and had always wondered what it would be like. *Bloody hell, I'm sitting here watching three complete strangers fuck and touch each other only a few metres away.* She snorted out a laugh. "I can't fucking believe this place exists."

Kris grinned then, the first genuine smile she'd given all evening. "I know! I feel like I'm sitting on the set of some porn movie, but in a really good way."

Some of the tension eased from Jody's body at Kris's words. "Yeah, I know what you mean. For once, I'm not feeling guilty about objectifying the half-naked women in front of me."

Kris laughed, then stood. "I need to pee. You going to be okay here?"

"Of course." Jody's hackles rose. "I can look after myself."

"You know that isn't what I meant." Kris stared her down. "I'm just taking account of your nerves about being here."

Chastened, Jody swallowed hard before speaking. "Sorry."

Kris nodded, her mouth set in a tight line. "Be back in a minute."

Jody watched her go, knowing she'd been wrong to snap. She sighed. Ever since the accident, she'd been carrying around a whole fuck ton of feelings, loads of them not good. Sometimes her mouth still got the better of her. And the last person who deserved to be on the wrong end of it all was Kris.

She turned back to face the room. A new woman had appeared, standing along the wall a short distance from the threesome, who were still going strong. The newcomer was gorgeous. Like, supermodel gorgeous: long legs, curvy hips, ample breasts, and flowing brown hair that caressed her bare shoulders. She wore a tight sleeveless top, maybe pink in colour—it was hard to tell in the room's low light—and a pair of jeans that looked like they'd been painted on.

Yum.

The curvy woman caught Jody's eye and smiled, an expression that promised so much; even Jody could read that, despite her long-term absence from any kind of dating or hooking-up scene. She swallowed, her pulse racing and perspiration forming in the small of her back. Her feet tapped a rhythm on the footrest of the stool, and she shifted in her seat a tad to ease the pressure that had built, seemingly out of nowhere, in her pussy.

The woman lifted her chin and eased her shoulders back, pushing her breasts out.

Jody swallowed once more, then, without overthinking it, even though her heart pounded in her ears, she slowly slid off the stool, checking her balance with every move. Once she was standing, she took a deep breath before walking across the room.

When she reached her, she made sure to keep her left side turned away a little. She had no idea if the woman had already seen the big gap where Jody's left arm used to be, but she'd rather not make it obvious—not right away, not before she'd even had the chance to talk to her. "Hey."

"Hey yourself." The woman looked her up and down. "Haven't seen you here before."

Jody dumbly shook her head.

"I'm Mel. What's your name, handsome?"

"Jody."

Mel ran one fingertip down the centre of Jody's chest. "Nice to meet you, Jody."

No one had touched her, not like that, in about eighteen months. It was the simplest of touches, but because of what it meant, of the barriers it broke, it set her body on fire. She exhaled sharply, aware of nerve endings tingling and sizzling all over her skin, and especially down her phantom arm. It was almost too much, too soon. "Can I…can I get you a drink?" Her voice was nothing more than a rasp.

Mel smiled. "I'd rather not wait." She made to place her hands on Jody's hips.

Jody took half a step back, even as her body yearned towards that touch. "Sorry, I…I need to go a little slower."

"Yeah?" Mel looked puzzled. Perhaps, with her looks, no one had never not wanted to jump her bones the minute they were offered the chance.

Not feeling the need to explain, certainly not to a stranger, Jody simply nodded. "It's okay if you'd rather wait for someone else."

"No, I think I'll take a drink from you. You've intrigued me." Mel tilted her head. "But I think I'll take something else to go first."

Before Jody could do anything about it, even if she'd wanted to, Mel ran her hands up around Jody's neck and pulled her head down.

The kiss was hard, almost bruising. Mel's lips crushed against Jody's, the heat of them searing through her. Even though her body somehow froze, her mouth didn't; she returned the kiss with equal force, revelling in the soft plumpness of Mel's lips as they moved over hers.

When Mel licked at her bottom lip, Jody gladly opened her mouth, and pushed her own tongue deep into Mel's mouth. It felt good. Sort of. While most of her was engaged in her first kiss in so long, a smaller part of her admitted it felt a little… off.

Mel was hot; of course she was. So why did Jody have the overwhelming urge to back away? She was kissing a hot woman! The first one she'd kissed in ages, and the first one she'd kissed since she'd become physically less than her former self. Mel either hadn't twigged about the arm, or wasn't bothered, and either way suited Jody just fine. Didn't it?

Jody pulled back, gulping in air.

Mel grinned. "Uh-huh. I'll have a white wine, thanks."

Nodding, still breathing heavily, Jody backed off a step or two. There was a part of her that wanted to buy Mel the wine and then just walk away, and she couldn't begin to understand why. This was what she wanted, wasn't it? A chance to get physical with someone who she would never have to see again. So how come all she wanted to do was run away?

When she turned away from Mel towards the bar, Kris was back on her stool at the table in the centre of the room, staring at her. Her expression was unreadable.

Jody stepped over to her. "You okay?"

Kris's gaze flicked to Mel and back again. "Yeah. All good."

Jody grinned, despite the swirl of strange thoughts and emotions churning on her inside. "Her name's Mel."

Kris looked Mel's way once more. "She looks just your type." The words were delivered in a flat monotone that unsettled Jody.

She dipped her head to try to catch Kris's eye. "I'm just going to the bar to get her a drink. You want something too?"

Kris closed her eyes for a moment, then eased off the stool. "You know what, I'm good. I…I'm really happy for you, okay? But I need to leave. You stay here as long as you like. Message me when you're done, and I'll pick you up."

"Wait, what? Where are you going?" What the hell was going on?

"I don't know. Maybe I'll go to MacDonald's or something." Kris walked a few paces towards the bar.

Jody strode after her. "But… I don't understand."

"I know you don't. But that's okay." Kris gestured to where Mel waited. "This is what you wanted. You've done it, broken through whatever was holding you back. And that's great. I'm pleased for you. I just can't—" She stepped to the side to let a couple walk past her and kept herself turned away from Jody once they'd passed.

Jody's heart thudded once more, but this time not from excitement. Something was very wrong here. "Kris, you're kind of scaring me. What's going on?" When Kris didn't respond, she took hold of her wrist and tugged her round. "Please, tell me. You've been off, not yourself, for a while now. And I know you don't like to talk about feelings and all that crap, but you're my best mate, and if there's something wrong, I want to help you."

Kris yanked her hand away; her eyes blazed with something close to anger, and Jody recoiled in shock. "Just leave it, okay? It's nothing you can do anything about. It's crystal clear you're back in the game and got the kind of woman who's just what you like. Go get her drink and get back to her before you lose your chance."

"Fuck that!" None of this made sense. She stepped into Kris's body space and glared at her. "Something's fucked-up here, and I want to know what. And fuck her, she can wait for her wine or whatever. You're my best friend. Tell me what's wrong so I can—"

Kris grabbed her by the hips and swung her round. It nearly threw her off balance completely, but Kris's hands and arms were strong and kept her upright even as she then pushed Jody backwards.

As her back thudded against the wall, Jody let out a grunt. "What the—?"

Kris's blue eyes blazed, but this time not from anger.

Just as Jody figured out what she saw in them, Kris leaned in and kissed her. She kissed her as if Jody was something she'd craved for a long, *long* time, with a hunger that sent a shockwave rippling down Jody's body.

Her lips were hot, and softer than Jody would ever have imagined, and her hands, gripping Jody's hips so tightly, were strong, claiming Jody's body as hers. It was a kiss she would never have expected, not in a million years, but now it had started she wondered how she'd lived without it. There was a tiny part of her mind exploding with confusion that it was *Kris* kissing her, but the rest of her surrendered to the power of Kris's mouth, her hands, her lithe yet strong body pressed up against Jody, keeping her pinned to the wall.

When Kris pushed the tip of her tongue between Jody's lips, she thought she was in danger of self-combusting. How did that small action, something she'd shared with so many other women in the past, have so much more effect on her because it was Kris doing it? She moaned and opened her mouth, letting Kris in, her pussy clenching in excitement at the feel of Kris's tongue probing deep into her mouth. *This is crazy. She's my best friend. She's butch. I've never fancied another butch in my entire life! What is going on?* Then Kris's tongue began the most incredible stroking, and all her thoughts scattered like leaves on the wind.

Jody reached her hand up and cupped the back of Kris's head. The shaved hair felt incredible under her fingertips, soft yet filled with sharp little edges that tickled her palm. She was so used to running her fingers through long locks that it was disconcerting to find nothing more than stubble. Even as she enjoyed the wondrous things Kris's mouth did to her, she felt as if the world had buckled beneath her, as if there'd been some kind of earthquake here in the heart of Manchester.

Kris groaned and pressed her hips even more into Jody.

"What's going on?" a voice said nearby.

They broke apart, chests heaving for breath.

Kris looked shell-shocked, her eyes wide and glazed.

Jody didn't know what she felt, other than surprisingly—hugely—turned on. She turned her head to find Mel standing nearby, her arms folded across her chest. "Mel," she managed to croak out.

"I thought you and me were going to get something started." Mel pointed at Jody. "But now you're with her? Or were you after a threesome? Because I'm not totally against that idea."

"No!" Jody and Kris both said, then looked at each other and burst out laughing.

"Well, fucking excuse me." Mel's tone was scathing.

"Mel, look, I'm sorry." Jody sucked in a deep breath. "This… Something…" She gazed into Kris's face, filled with wonder once again at what had just transpired—and what might yet come. "Sorry, but I'm not available. I didn't mean to lead you on."

Mel huffed out an annoyed breath, then stomped away, swearing loudly.

Jody laughed, then became very aware of the feel of Kris's arms around her, the press of her hips, the heat that simmered between them. "What the actual fuck, Kris?"

Kris let go with one hand to rub it over her face; her cheeks were flushed deep pink. "Um, yeah." She exhaled, her warm breath washing over Jody's forehead. "I'm sorry. I should never have just grabbed you like that."

Jody snorted. "Well, it seems I didn't mind." She shook her head. "This is just…bizarre."

Kris frowned, and started to ease back.

"Wait, wait. Not so fast." God, Kris felt good wrapped up against her. Way better than she would ever have thought. No way did she want that feeling to go away any time soon. *What the hell is happening to me?* "It's bizarre, but I like it."

"Really?" The hope in Kris's eyes made something lurch deep in Jody's belly.

"Yeah. A lot." Her own cheeks heated at the admission. "But I don't understand. Where did this come from? What does it mean?" *And what do I want it to be?*

Kris bit her bottom lip; the sexiness of the action nearly made Jody whimper. "I kind of realised a couple of months ago. I didn't have a clue what to do about it. Figured it might just go away if I ignored it, but that didn't work because we just spend all our time together and…" She sighed, then stood up a little straighter. "I feel…things for you. Things I never meant to share with you because I know I'm not remotely your type. I mean, shit, you're not really mine, are you? But those feelings are there, and when I saw you kissing her just now, it was like something kind of snapped inside me."

It was the most Jody had ever heard Kris talk about feelings and emotions. It was unsettling in its unfamiliarity but in a way that spread a warmth through her that had nothing to do with their proximity. Kris had feelings for *her*. Kris, who'd known her for so long, since before Jody became less than she'd previously been.

She could imagine Kris rolling her eyes at that thought.

Every day since Jody had lost the arm, Kris had calmly yet firmly tried to convince Jody that losing half a limb didn't make her any less of a person, any less of the person she'd been before. Shit, had Kris had feelings for her back then, before the accident? Was that why she'd worked so hard to prove to Jody she was whole?

Jody stared up at her friend, the one who'd been there for her every step of the way in this journey. The one, Jody now realised, who'd been paramount in her thoughts every day of the last year. The first person she wanted to talk to at the start of each day, the last person she wanted to talk to at the end of each night. She blinked. *Oh my God. It's* her. *She's been here this whole time, right in front of me. How did I not see it?*

The revelation lifted something, broke through one layer of hurt and then another and another. It seared through all of her protections and boundaries.

She looked at Kris then—really looked at her, with fresh eyes and perspective—and smiled so widely it hurt her jaw. "Thank you."

Kris's eyes narrowed. "For what?" Her voice was a nervous croak.

"Everything." And she leaned up and kissed Kris, using her one hand to pull Kris's head down so she could deepen the kiss to the point of bruising. Because she needed to *feel* now. Feel Kris and this incredible heat they seemed to generate within milliseconds of their lips touching.

Kris's loud groan was music to her ears.

Jody stroked Kris's tongue with her own, and Kris ground her hips into hers. Jody made to move her left arm, to wrap Kris fully in her arms, and nearly screamed with frustration at the realisation that she couldn't, even though her phantom fingers tingled at the prospect. But then, just as her anger and bitterness rose, it was as if Kris had read her mind: she used both of her arms to wrap around Jody as close as she could manage, bringing their bodies together into the tight embrace Jody craved.

It was the perfect alternative, and her whole body quivered with the sensations it engendered. And it wasn't only physical; Kris's understanding, here tonight and every day in the last year, made Jody's heart fill with things she couldn't name but which felt so fucking right.

Kris eased back from the kiss, biting gently on Jody's bottom lip as she did so. "Holy shit," she whispered.

Jody laughed, and her hand clutched convulsively at Kris's neck. "Yeah."

"I had no idea we could be this good. I mean, I hoped, but..."

"Is it bad that I didn't even consider it?" Jody swallowed. "I just never saw you that way."

Kris shrugged. "Why would you? Never mind all the shit you've had to deal with this past year, but you and I were in the friend zone, weren't we? Why would either of us, both so into those long-haired femmes, think this was possible?"

"But you did, at some point."

"Yeah." Kris gave her a lazy smile. "It wasn't like it was a big light bulb moment, though. Like, you didn't do something amazing one day and I swooned."

Jody snorted. "I find that hard to believe. Everyone swoons with me around." God, it felt good to joke like she used to, to have even a hint of her previous cockiness.

Kris pinched her shoulder blade. "Ha fucking ha."

They kissed again, tenderly this time, lingering in the feel of each other's lips, their tongues brushing lightly.

Fuck, I'm so wet. Kris kissed like a fucking dream. She very nearly rolled her eyes into the back of her head. *Don't go getting all gushy, for fuck's sake.*

They pulled apart once more.

"So, what now?" Kris's voice didn't tremble, but there was a hint of nerves in her eyes and in the tightness around her mouth.

"Well, more of that would be good." Jody smirked.

Kris smiled weakly. "Yeah, okay, but I meant, you know, longer term."

Yeah, and I knew that, but I still had to crack a joke, didn't I? Fuckwit. She knew why, of course: classic defence mechanism. Kris offered her something that could be amazing. Life-changing. And did so knowing everything there was to know about Jody—the arm, the psychological impact of that, and the steps Jody was still going through to come to terms with it.

Kris knew it all—and wanted Jody anyway. Wanted *them* to be something.

Jody cleared her throat. "How about longer term we move from the friend zone into the girlfriend zone? Starting now."

Kris's nod was slow, her smile wide. "That sounds good to me."

Happiness wasn't something Jody had felt much of in the last twelve months, but now she wanted to laugh out loud with it. "Jesus, I can't believe how this evening's turned out." She shook her head in wonder.

"I know. Kind of nuts, huh?"

"It really is. I mean, I walked in here about an hour ago thinking I might, maybe, possibly, find someone for a quick shag up against a wall, and now look where I am." She looked pointedly down at their bodies pressed close together and grinned.

"Well, you can still get that shag, if you like."

Jody startled. "What?" Surely Kris didn't mean she should just go off and find—

"I don't know about you, but I'm as horny as fuck." Kris's eyes smouldered. "If you want our first time to be all romantic and all that, then we can head out of here right now back to my place. But you've got me so fucking wet from kissing you, I can't wait to get inside you and fuck you the way I've dreamed of doing for months now. And I want to do that. Here. Now."

Heat raged through Jody's veins at the words, and her clit leaped to attention. She nodded because words were impossible now that her brain and body were on fire.

Kris didn't smile, or nod, or even squeeze Jody a little tighter. She simply kissed her once more, this time with all the passion of the first kiss. And just like that first one, the hunger the kiss expressed made Jody's body ache with wanting to assuage that appetite.

She ran her hand down Kris's back to the bottom of her T-shirt and slipped her fingers underneath. The skin she found was hot and so smooth beneath her touch it nearly took her breath away. She pushed higher, roughly stroking as much of Kris's back as she could, trying not to think too hard about how much better this would be with two hands. This was her new reality, and she just had to get used to it. Then she ran her hand lower, into the back of Kris's jeans. It was tight, but she was determined. With a little wriggle she managed it. She clasped hold of Kris's ass and squeezed it.

Kris grunted, undid her jeans, and shoved them halfway down her hips, which gave Jody considerably more room to manoeuvre.

She took full advantage, cupping Kris's ridiculously tight ass cheek and kneading it. Jody had a thing about asses and knew without a doubt she was going to enjoy getting to intimately know this one. Hopefully that thought would be well received. "This okay?"

Kris caught her eye and grinned. "Definitely. Play all you want down there."

"When we have more room, I will, don't you worry." She shifted position, bending her knees a tad, and worked her finger in between the cheeks of Kris's ass.

Kris gasped and stared at her, pulling her bottom lip between her teeth once more.

Jody kept her gaze locked on Kris's as she ran the tip of her index finger down over the tightly puckered hole she sought.

Kris's eyes rolled shut and her breathing quickened.

"You like that?" Jody stroked back and forth.

"Holy fuck, yes." Kris opened her eyes. "But I'll need lube for anything else. And anyway, I'm supposed to be fucking you, remember?"

Jody grinned but withdrew her hand. "As long as we can come back to that sometime."

"Definitely." Kris pressed forward and kissed her again, shoving her tongue into Jody's mouth. More wetness flooded Jody's shorts.

God, the things this woman could do with her tongue. Jody's brain short-circuited at that thought; oral wasn't something she normally allowed anyone to do to her, preferring to be a giver rather than a taker. But something told her Kris would have her tongue on Jody's clit before the weekend was over and that she'd willingly open her legs wide for it.

Holy shit, what is she doing to me?

Kris eased her hold on Jody, but only so she could reach up for the buttons on Jody's shirt. "This needs to at least come undone." She opened her heavy-lidded eyes for a moment. "I'll understand if you don't want to take it off completely, but I need to be able to get underneath your clothes. I want to touch your skin. Your breasts."

Her nipples sprang to attention at the words. "Undo it."

Kris came back for another kiss as her hands moved once more.

A few moments later, they both had their wish, and Jody pushed into Kris's touch. Kris swept her hands up Jody's torso, underneath her now slightly damp T-shirt. When she reached Jody's small breasts, braless as always, and cupped them in her warm hands, they both groaned into each other's mouths.

"Feels so fucking good." Kris's voice rasped with her need, setting off more tiny explosions of desire throughout Jody's body. She pinched Jody's nipples, softly at first, then harder until Jody gasped into her mouth. "Too much?" Kris asked.

"No! Need it." Jody could only grind the words out between gritted teeth. "Harder." She was unravelling underneath Kris's touch, but didn't care. She trusted Kris to take her as far as she wanted, further, probably, than anyone else had, but that was okay.

Kris obliged, rolling and pulling at Jody's small nipples with her fingertips.

Jody moved her mouth to Kris's ear. "Don't hold back. Give it to me. Give me everything." Because, yes, that's what she wanted. Everything Kris could give her.

The groan that escaped Kris's chest made Jody tremble as Kris grabbed her breasts and squeezed hard, mashing them into her ribcage, moving them around in hard circles then grasping her nipples. She pulled so hard, Jody whimpered with the pleasure-pain combination.

"Like that?" Kris rasped. "You like it hard like that?"

Jody humped her groin against Kris's, and Kris's wicked laugh filled the tiny gap between their faces. "Oh yeah, you're ready, aren't you?" Kris moved one hand downwards to open the zip on Jody's jeans and tug them down a little. "Ready to be fucked, aren't you?"

Jesus H. Christ. Kris dirty-talking had to be the hottest fucking thing she'd ever heard. She didn't think she'd ever been so desperate for someone's fingers to find her. "Fuck, yes."

"Yeah, you're gonna take whatever I give you, aren't you?"

Jody whimpered once more and nodded furiously.

And then Kris moved her hand again, this time into Jody's boxers, down over her thatch of hair, and without any hesitation ran her fingers into the wetness that awaited.

Jody was a little embarrassed by how soaked she was, how obvious it telegraphed her need, but that feeling didn't linger—Kris's extended moan, her breathing heavy against Jody's lips, told her she had nothing to be concerned about.

"Jesus, you feel so fucking good." Kris's gaze locked on Jody's as she ran two fingers either side of Jody's clit to her entrance, then back again.

"Oh, fuck!"

Kris repeated the motion. Then again, this time a little faster and harder.

"Need you inside," Jody managed to pant out, not pulling her gaze away; it was hard. She was in danger of losing herself completely in Kris's heated expression, but the connection, the pull, was simply too strong to resist.

"Whatever you want." Kris's voice was choked. "Whatever you want." She slipped her fingers past Jody's clit once more, but this time when she reached the entrance to her cunt, she pushed one finger slowly inside.

It was good but not enough. Not nearly enough. "More." Jody didn't recognise her own voice. The demanding need in it was something new.

Kris pulled out, then re-entered her with two fingers, not being gentle about it, pushing as deep as she could go.

"Yes," Jody hissed, clutching at Kris's back, digging her fingernails in, glad for Kris's body pressing her close to the wall to keep her from falling.

Kris pressed her forehead to Jody's and worked her hand within the confines of Jody's boxers, pulling out of her almost completely, then plunging her fingers back into Jody's cunt.

It was incredible. Kris filled her, stretched her with her long, strong fingers. Her movement was perfect, keeping it slow but hard, exactly how Jody liked it. She moved with Kris, pushing down, impaling herself on those fingers every time they went deep, shamelessly humping Kris's hand as she panted in her ear. "Fuck me. Fuck me hard."

Kris's forehead dampened with sweat. Her mouth found Jody's for another crushing kiss. "I want to make you come. What do you need?"

She'd never get the right angle, Jody knew that. She'd spent enough time learning her body, what worked and what didn't, to know she'd only get frustrated if Kris tried. "Can I—can I do it?" The grin Kris threw her at that was so dirty, it made Jody laugh. "You like that idea?"

"Fuck, yeah. I can't think of anything hotter." Kris slowly nodded, her pupils dilated.

"I can. But we'll save that for later."

Kris laughed, and Jody marvelled at how at ease they were with each other while Kris had her fingers inside her and they were fucking in a room full of strangers. *I guess this was always what we were, though. Thank God Kris said something tonight; I don't want to miss another day of this.*

She let go of Kris's back and smiled in gratitude when Kris changed her body position to allow Jody to slip her arm between them.

"What do you need from me?" Kris gazed at her, her eyes saying so much that Jody wasn't quite ready to acknowledge.

But probably one day soon.

"Just keep fucking me. You filling me like that is fucking amazing." It was easy to vocalise the physical; actually, it was all she could deal with right now. And that was okay. Tonight, it seemed, was just about that, about getting beyond this first big hurdle.

"I have zero problem with that." Kris pushed inside again and began a slow and even rhythm.

Jody took a moment to enjoy that sensation once more, leaning forward to kiss Kris, to bite and nibble on her lips, to push her tongue deep into Kris's mouth just to hear her moan again. Then, with their mouths still fused, Jody slipped her hand into her boxers and ran the tip of her middle finger over her hard and throbbing clit.

Fuck, I don't think this will take long. She wished it would, wished she could drag it out for hours because all of it felt so fucking good.

"Holy shit," Kris whispered, looking down between them.

Jody followed her gaze. Their hands moved in unison inside her shorts, and she totally got what had Kris so worked up; both of them working her cunt and clit together was as hot as fuck.

Kris's fingers plunged deeper and faster. "When you fuck my ass," she ground out, "I want it like this. Hard and fast. Take me hard and fast."

"Fuck!" Jody worked her finger into that magic little spot, just to the right side of her clit, that spot she'd mastered only last night as the sure-fire way to bring herself to a climax. She wasn't prepared, though. Not for *this* climax. Not for how it would feel to come with Kris inside her, to have Kris pressed up against her, her mouth hungry on hers.

It ripped her apart, then put her back together. It was heat and wetness and something far more than physical. She arched so much, her head hit the wall behind her. Her cunt clenched around Kris's fingers while the finger she kept on her clit drew every last drop out of the orgasm. It was too much; it wasn't enough.

Kris's other arm held her tight around her back, keeping her upright. She pressed into Jody, kissing her forehead, over her eyes, her nose, her cheeks. "Jody," she whispered. "Holy fuck."

"Yeah. I know." Jody still had her eyes shut tight, still had unbelievable sensations rippling over her skin and inside her cunt. Kris was tight within her, but Jody wasn't ready for her to pull out. Not yet. "Stay," she murmured.

Kris kissed her, soft and slow. "Yes. Always."

CHAPTER 7

MANDY

MANDY ATTACHED THE BUTTERFLY TO the back of her last stud earring, then straightened and looked at her image in the mirror. It didn't look too bad. The grey trousers she'd bought earlier that week were a flattering cut, smoothing out some of the softness that had settled on her hips and around her waist in the last few years. The off-white top, made of a faux silk material that actually felt delicious on her skin, had a wide neckline and batwing sleeves, a style she'd long known suited her.

She didn't get to dress up that often these days. Her circle of friends had never been big but had dwindled further as the passing years inevitably took people in different directions. And with her work at the club dominating her weekends, her social engagements were usually during the week, fitting around other people's work hours and family commitments. A chance to dress up for a proper meal out on a Saturday evening was a rare but special event.

"What am I doing?" She asked the question out loud to her reflected image and only felt a little silly about doing so. Then she blew out a breath and stepped back from the mirror. It was just dinner.

Ah yes, but…

A quick glance at her watch told her she still had plenty of time, which was a shame because that gave her mind more time to fuck with her. She walked through to the hallway to hunt for her dressy black shoes.

It's just dinner. It's not a date. Neither of them had called their get-togethers that. And that was fine, wasn't it? She sighed. Except, deep down, she'd started to wonder if they really were dates, and if they were, what that might mean.

Of course they're dates! The woman's travelling up here from Brighton on a regular basis purely to see you*!*

Yes, that was true. But Laura hadn't given any hint that she wanted anything more between them than just the pleasure of two acquaintances who enjoyed each other's company.

They had a lot in common, they'd discovered. As Laura owned a landscaping business, she could relate to the trials and tribulations of running her own company, just like Mandy. They shared their love of modern art, of course, but also crime novels, Indian food, and a good, full-bodied red wine. Their different music tastes were a source of amusement—for God's sake, she liked Abba!—but their mutual love for Meryl Streep and Helen Mirren had led to them making tentative plans for a trip to the cinema one day soon, either here in Manchester or on Mandy's next visit to Brighton, which they'd already pencilled in for a month's time.

And, of course, Laura was *very* attractive. Mandy tamped down the flutter of excitement that stirred in her belly at the memory of how delicious Laura had looked the last time they met. The lightweight, blue sweater over bootleg Levi's was a simple but oh-so-flattering look on her sturdy frame. Her green eyes changed colour intensity to match her moods and captivated Mandy. One minute, as she laughed over a shared joke, they would sparkle like a pale green amber, then turn to an emerald colour when discussing something serious or painful.

They'd shared much already, a lot of it personal—something Mandy had found both easy and a tad alarming. Laura still grieved for Kelly, Mandy knew, but had moved past the worst of it. And knowing Laura's story, Mandy had finally told her about Rebecca. No one had ever known the full story, but telling Laura was easier than she'd imagined, even as it had unsettled her. She felt exposed by her willingness to open up to Laura, and it wasn't as if she could even blame Laura for that. Mandy had volunteered information, told stories to Laura she'd never shared with anyone other than Rebecca.

What does it mean? And why am I so nervous about meeting her again this evening? She should never have said yes, nor arranged for Nina to open the club on her own that night and leave her with no excuse not to go to dinner with Laura. *What was I thinking?*

Still, at least she did have the safety outlet of the club. She had already told Laura she had to be there by ten at the latest before it got too busy. Laura had merely suggested they meet for an earlier meal at six thirty so they wouldn't feel rushed.

So here she was, at a little after six on a Saturday evening, getting ready to meet Laura once more, and excited at the prospect, despite all her doubts and fears.

She slipped on her shoes and looked around for her handbag. Car and house keys, wallet, phone—check. The weather, still warm for September, meant she only needed a light jacket, which she hung over her arm for now. Then she sucked in a deep breath and headed out the door.

The restaurant, a classy French-Moroccan fusion place only about ten minutes' drive from the club, was already quite full by the time Mandy walked in. Her reserved table was off to the side, near a window that looked out over a small green-filled square.

"Lovely, thank you," she said to the waitress who'd led her to the table.

"Can I get you some water while you wait?"

"Perfect. Still, please."

The waitress smiled and strode off.

Mandy focused on breathing, slow and sure, to calm her nerves. *Come on, you're fifty-five! Get a grip.*

But when Laura appeared, walking with her easy stride across the room, a wide smile on her face, Mandy's heart thumped wildly. *Oh my God, she looks stunning.*

Laura wore a dark-grey shirt, the cuffs and collar edged with silver piping. And the shirt was tucked into black leather trousers that looked as if they'd been handmade just for her, fitting perfectly *everywhere*. Black boots that climbed halfway up her calves finished the look and left Mandy wondering if the restaurant owned any smelling salts because she was surely about to swoon.

"Hi," Laura said as she pulled out her chair.

"Hello." *Oh, thank God, I can talk.* "You look incredible." *Oh shit, why did I say that?*

Laura paused halfway through sitting and gave Mandy a sensual smile. "Thank you. So do you, but, then, you always do." She sat and gazed across the table.

God, when she looks at me like that… "Thank you." She held Laura's gaze for a moment, then distracted herself by picking up her menu. "So, how was your journey, and how was your day?"

"Well, my day has pretty much been my journey—there were delays with the first train, which meant I missed all my other connections. I only arrived about an hour and a half ago."

"Oh no! So you've had no time to visit that exhibition you wanted to see?"

Laura smiled ruefully. "Nope. But hey, there'll be other times." She gave Mandy a look that could only be described as hopeful.

Mandy nodded before she could overthink things. "There will."

"Good. Now, I'm starving! Let's order."

The three hours they had together flew by, and Mandy had no trouble admitting to herself that she was sad about that. As she followed Laura out of the restaurant, her gaze dropped to the beautiful view of Laura's ass encased in the leather.

Down, girl.

They reached the corner where Mandy would need to turn off for her car. She presumed Laura had taken the tram, and if so, this would be where they parted; the tram stop was in the opposite direction. She didn't want the evening to end, but she had to get to work.

"Where are you parked?" Laura asked, stopping at the corner.

"That way." Mandy pointed. "Do you want a lift back to your hotel? It's pretty much on the way to the club." Mandy's stomach lurched. "Oh, that's assuming you don't want to visit the club tonight, of course. Because, obviously, you can. You're more than welcome. Any time. Just like anyone else."

Stop babbling! She couldn't help it, though—the thought of Laura coming to the club and finding someone to play with for the evening made jealousy, thick as molasses, fill her veins. She finally acknowledged she *wanted* Laura. Wanted to have more than the occasional lunch with interesting and amusing conversation. Wanted so much more.

Laura looked away for a moment, then turned back to Mandy and stepped close. Very close. The heat from her body made goose bumps break out down Mandy's arms.

"No, I don't want to visit the club." Laura's eyes had darkened to a jade colour. "I want…" She rolled her bottom lip between her teeth. "The thing is, I really just want you."

Mandy's mind went blank. *Did she just say she wants me?* Her skin tingled.

"I don't want to ruin this friendship we've found," Laura said, keeping her gaze locked on Mandy's, "but I have to be honest: I want more than friendship. I didn't think I'd ever want a relationship again, not after Kelly. But I'm really attracted to you and I'm already starting to have feelings for you, and I'd love us to give it a try if you're interested. I've been waiting for the right moment to say it, and I don't know if now is it, but, well, here I am—saying it."

Mandy's heart, the heart she thought had been broken beyond repair after Rebecca died, skipped a joyful beat. "I'm so glad you're here saying it, because I think I want that too." Her voice was thick, her emotions tightening her throat.

One corner of Laura's mouth quirked up. "You *think*?"

"It's—well, it's that—you see, I've never really done this. You know, a relationship. I'm not sure how to, and I'm a bit scared of it, actually."

Laura's gaze bore into hers. "But you feel the same way about me as I do about you?"

Her cheeks heated, but Mandy held her chin up. "Yes, I do. But can you take me on, knowing I'm scared and I might fuck this all up just because I'm going to be stumbling my way through whatever we have?" She had to be honest with her; they were too old for playing games and wasting each other's time.

Laura's smile shot heat all the way down to Mandy's toes. "We can stumble through it together. I'm still healing; you know that. But I also know I'm ready to move on. So we'll just go slow, yes? See where it takes us?" She gently took Mandy's hand.

Mandy exhaled and grasped Laura's hand tight. "Sounds good to me."

"Good." Laura inched closer and slid her other hand around Mandy's waist.

The touch stirred things in Mandy. They'd never even hugged before now, so to be in Laura's embrace set off tingles all over her body. And there was desire there, yes, but there was also something more, something she wasn't sure how to name. Whatever it was, the mix of sensations that skittered over her was good—of that much she was sure.

"It's twenty-five years since we last kissed." Laura's voice was a husky whisper. "I'd love to know what it feels like to kiss you again."

Mandy could only nod; the power of the heat between them was too much for words.

Laura closed the distance. Her lips were soft on Mandy's to begin with, which was delicious, but the touch only made Mandy want more.

She wrapped her arms around Laura, pressed their bodies together, and devoured Laura's mouth.

Laura moaned and gave back just as good as she got, then broke their kiss for air a minute later. "Okay," she said, in between heavy breaths, "thanks for reminding me."

Mandy laughed and poked her in the bicep. They stared at each other, both smiling widely.

"I think I'm going to walk to my hotel. It's a nice night, and a walk might be just what I need to lose some of this amazing energy I seem to have right now." She stepped back and shook out her arms, an almost childlike smile on her face. "Brunch tomorrow? Call me when you're up and awake?"

"Definitely." Mandy wanted to pull her back in, wanted more kisses, more of…everything. *Maybe tomorrow.*

"And then we'll see how we go."

"We will."

They shared one last gentle kiss, then said their goodbyes.

Mandy turned back as she reached her car.

Laura still stood on the corner where they'd kissed, watching her, a big smile on her face. She waved once, then strode off.

Mandy got behind the wheel and laughed out loud into the silence of her car. For the first time since the club had opened, right now, it was the last place she wanted to be.

CHAPTER 8

SUZANNE

"Tea's brewed!" Suzanne called up the stairs.

"Thanks!"

Suzanne smiled, knowing Joanna was probably rushing around their bedroom, trying to get dressed after inadvertently sleeping past the alarm. Thank God Suzanne had rushed upstairs to wake her once she'd realised she hadn't heard a peep out of her since her own shower.

"Stupid alarm," Joanna said as she walked into the kitchen tying a silk scarf around her neck. "Of all the days."

Suzanne handed her a cup of tea and kissed her quickly on the lips. "You've still got time, don't worry."

"I know, but you know I like my routine." Joanna popped a slice of bread into the toaster, then pulled the butter from the fridge.

"I do." Suzanne gave her a tender smile. Her wife was nothing if not a creature of habit. "So, remind me again: are you home early or late tonight?"

Joanna turned to face her fully, and Suzanne experienced that little zap of affection as she gazed at the woman she'd been with now for fifteen years. It had never died out, even if other aspects of their relationship had diminished.

"It's Friday, so it's eight o'clock finish after evening classes."

Shit, I should know that by now. "Yes, sorry. Of course."

Joanna quirked a smile at her, then focused her attention on her toast, buttering it quickly before taking a huge bite.

"How about if I have a nice hot bath waiting for you when you get home?" Suzanne edged over to her and wrapped her arms gently around her from behind. She nuzzled at Joanna's neck, where the soft strands that had escaped her ponytail tickled at her nose. "Maybe light some candles, pour some wine, and I'll join you in there. You know, both of us naked and warm, and..." She kissed the back of Joanna's neck, her arousal flaring at just the thought of touching Joanna intimately again. God knew it had been a while.

Joanna squirmed in her arms and turned, half a slice of toast still in one hand. "Um, probably not a good idea. I know I've got papers from yesterday's class still to grade, and I don't want to do them at the weekend because we wanted to visit that garden centre tomorrow, and then there's lunch with my parents on Sunday."

Suzanne worked hard to keep the disappointment from her face. "Of course. That makes sense." She kissed the end of Joanna's nose. "Now, eat your toast."

"Sorry," Joanna whispered, staring into Suzanne's eyes. "It seems lately all we do is work. I know...I know you're frustrated about us not, you know, having sex much these days."

Suzanne sighed. "I can't lie, I am a little." She ran her fingers over the beautiful column of Joanna's neck. "But I get it. You're now senior lecturer at the college, and you'll probably make head of department very soon. And that's fantastic. And my work has just exploded in the last two years, and both of those things mean we're both really tired all of the time."

"It's a poor excuse though, isn't it? Blaming work?" Joanna looked worried, her usual calm face creased with a deep frown.

God, I'm not ready to have the other part of this conversation. I haven't even figured it all out for myself. "I think it happens to a lot of people." It wasn't a lie. "Maybe we can make a special effort next weekend to make more time for us."

Joanna's frown deepened. "I've got that conference next weekend." She leaned in and kissed Suzanne, hard and fast. "But you're right, we should at least try."

Suzanne gave her one last squeeze, then stepped back before her face could betray her. "We will."

Joanna munched the last of her toast. "Okay, I need to go soon, but quickly, tell me how it's going with Jody?"

Suzanne sighed. "It's fine. You know I struggled with not saying anything last month about the anniversary, but that was great advice from you, as it really seemed to help her to just carry on as normal. Since then, she's been literally buzzing with energy. I haven't pried, but I think there's something going on outside of work that's really good."

"Well, that's great to hear."

"Yeah. Oh, and speaking of good things, I never got a chance to tell you this last night as we barely saw each other."

Joanna smiled ruefully. "I know, sorry again."

"No, no, that's not why I'm saying that. Anyway, the lovely news. You know Stephanie, the business analyst we've had on site for a few weeks now?"

Joanna nodded, then sipped at her tea.

"Well, she's engaged! Turned up yesterday wearing a very lovely diamond ring. Apparently, her girlfriend proposed, completely out of the blue, the night before. Stephanie says although they've been together not even two years yet, she's known Lou is the one for her since the night they first got together." Suzanne smiled as Joanna made a little *aw* sound. "I know! It's so lovely." She leaned in to kiss Joanna once more. "Made me remember proposing to you."

Joanna kissed her back, her lips hot from her tea. "Mm, that was a very lovely day."

"I love you."

"And I love you." Joanna glanced up at the kitchen clock. "But I have to go. I'm sorry."

"Okay. Have a great day, my love."

Joanna threw her that smile, the one that was filled with so much love and warmth, and Suzanne's heart fluttered just like it did every time it came her way. "You too. Bye."

Suzanne watched her leave, that little tingle of arousal still simmering between her legs. Being turned on by even the smallest of touches or kisses from Joanna had happened so many times over the last few months, she'd given up being surprised by it. She'd always had a good sexual appetite, or at least one she was happy with, but since hitting her mid-forties, that appetite seemed to have gone into overdrive.

Which had unfortunately coincided with a distinct drift into lesbian bed death for her and Joanna. It used to be so good. They'd made love at least once a week. Although they'd generally always used one of the same two or three positions, their knowledge of each other's bodies, built up over the years, had meant they'd each time both achieved a nicely satisfying orgasm—sometimes even two orgasms, when they had a whole evening to indulge.

Being honest with herself, Suzanne knew it wasn't just exhaustion from their jobs that got in the way. A big part of it was her changing desires, or needs, or whatever the hell they were—and her complete inability to talk to Joanna about it.

Her wife wasn't a prude; that word took things too far. But she was...embarrassed by sex? Yes, maybe that was it. Joanna came across as embarrassed to even admit she had desires in the first place. Their discussions about what they liked had happened way back in the early days of them dating and that was where they'd stopped. Suzanne knew about Joanna's past, understood her discomfort, and, really, it hadn't been an issue. The sex they'd had was good enough, and it hardly ever registered that it was so repetitive.

Until recently. Until Suzanne, aflame with sexual tension one weekend when Joanna was out of town visiting her elderly aunt, had stumbled across a kinky film on Amazon Prime. It was a male-female pairing, but it had been simple to imagine it being two women in the situation portrayed. And the situation, not something she'd ever considered before, had turned her on so much, she'd brought herself to two huge orgasms over the course of watching the film.

She flushed even now, thinking about it. But not with shame. She'd worked through her reactions to the scenes over the weeks afterwards, analysing what they'd done for her and why. And she was, for the most part, comfortable with admitting she wanted something similar and the reasons for it.

There was just no way, she thought, her wife would be up for it. Not in the way Suzanne wanted.

Joanna was all softness and gentleness, caring touches and caresses, whispered words of love. Lovely, but not remotely fitting the fantasy the film had planted in Suzanne's head—the fantasy that wouldn't let go and which kept Suzanne fired up in ways she never would have imagined even two years ago.

Getting off in the shower had become a regular part of her morning routine, the same ideas playing on a loop in her head as her left hand snaked between her wide-open thighs: Joanna standing over her, telling her what to do. Commanding her. Making Suzanne do her bidding. Taking away Suzanne's control, making her nothing more than a sexual toy for Joanna to enjoy at will. All the while, giving in to Joanna's every whim and desire, knowing her pleasure gave Joanna such pleasure.

Suzanne snorted out loud in the empty kitchen. *She'd run a mile if I asked.*

"Hey, babe, remind me again: does this shirt go in the thirty-degree wash or—" Suzanne frowned as Joanna jumped back in her seat at her desk in their small home office.

Joanna pressed a hand to her chest. "Wow, you gave me such a fright! You have your stealth mode on again."

"Sorry." Suzanne didn't think she'd been *that* quiet." Are you okay? Everything going okay with that research project?"

Joanna clicked a couple of times with her mouse, then smiled. "Oh, yes. All good."

Suzanne held out the white shirt. "So, thirty or forty?"

"That one's a thirty." Joanna ran a hand through her dark hair, which was loose tonight around her shoulders, Suzanne's favourite look. "And thank you for doing the washing."

"No problem." Suzanne blew her a kiss. "Got to have you looking all smart and proper for the weekend."

Joanna groaned. "Ugh, don't remind me."

"Hey, come on, you'll be fine. I know you're nervous, but every time you do one of these things you go in terrified, then come back glowing from all you learned."

"I know, I know. I just…" Joanna shook her head, and her gaze dropped. "I just wish I had more of your confidence. You can take charge of any situation just by breathing. Me, I'm lurking in the darkest corner and hoping no one will notice me."

Suzanne dropped the shirt on the floor—who cared, it was dirty already—and walked quickly around the desk. She wrapped her arms around Joanna and pulled her into her chest. "Hey, I've seen you at events, and you are brilliant, you hear me? Yes, you're not as bold and brash as I am, but that's just not you, is it?"

"No." Joanna's voice was muffled against Suzanne's abdomen. "I hate it."

Suzanne kissed the top of her wife's head, her heart near to bursting with pain at how down Joanna sounded. "Oh, my love. Come on. Just because you're not like me doesn't mean what you are is less, or wrong. You're brilliant. You're a fantastic lecturer and tutor, and you really, *really* know your stuff. That's why you've been invited to this conference in the first place, because you're that good! They know how lucky they are to have you."

"I suppose so." Joanna pulled back a little and smiled weakly up at Suzanne. "Thanks for the pep talk."

Taking Joanna's face in her hands, Suzanne gave her the biggest smile she could manage. "Any time, my love. Now, come on, back to that research and get yourself totally prepped to wow them on Saturday morning." She kissed her soundly, then let go of her face.

Joanna's gaze drifted back to her laptop. "Yes, research."

"Need anything? Tea? Wine? Something stronger?" It was a Wednesday night, but what the hell?

This time Joanna's smile seemed genuine. "Thanks, but no." She swivelled in her chair to face her desk once more. "I'm good."

Suzanne blew her one more kiss, then picked up the shirt and headed back to the kitchen.

Joanna's self-doubts clutched at Suzanne's heart every time they came to the fore. Her wife *was* brilliant at her job; she hadn't lied about that. But she also knew Joanna probably would have been up for head of department five years sooner if she'd had just an ounce more confidence. The conference she would attend at the weekend was a very big deal, and to have been invited as a keynote speaker was a huge honour. She knew Joanna knew that on some level, but her fears blocked the positivity of what her appearance meant. And there was nothing Suzanne could do other than say all the right things to try to bolster her wife up before she left on Friday morning.

She exhaled a long breath as she shoved the washing into the machine. She'd never begrudged being the strong one in the relationship, but sometimes… Unbidden, her mind went to her fantasy again.

Joanna taking charge, being strong. Suzanne being allowed to let go, to not have all the answers, to instead simply do what Joanna told her to, however kinky Joanna wanted it. That was the crux of the fantasy, wasn't it? Complete role reversal of their everyday life.

And therefore so unlikely ever to happen.

Porn Hub was eye-opening, to say the least. Suzanne knew she'd only last about another two minutes—some things she really could have gone the rest of her life without seeing. She wasn't even sure now why she'd started looking, other than that she was on her own in the house on a Saturday night, feeling horny and missing her wife. Oh, and she'd had two glasses of wine, so was definitely on the mellow side.

Halfway through the second glass, she'd had this great idea of trying to find the female equivalent of the kind of scene that film had portrayed. Of course, there was nothing like it in the mainstream stuff on Netflix or Amazon, at least not that she could find. Some internet searching had led her to an article on a magazine's website discussing porn made for women, either by women or by companies determined to offer something more in tune with women's ideas of what porn should be. And that had led her to one channel on Porn Hub where real-life queer women filmed themselves up to all sorts of things from vanilla to totally kinky.

She closed the video she'd only opened thirty seconds previously—she didn't need a man involved in her female fantasy, thank you very much. Next up was a link to a British couple who ran their own site. She downed a gulp of wine, then clicked the link and perused the menu. Nothing about the titles of their ten self-made films hinted at the kind of scene she'd like to watch, even though it did look as if they'd spent a lot of time making good quality films.

Her frustration threatened to boil over into launching her laptop across the room. "I cannot be the only woman who wants to watch another woman being dominated," she muttered, grabbing for her glass again. *Or wants it for herself,* was the follow-up thought she didn't voice out loud.

After tossing back the last of the wine, she scrolled back to the top of the screen, ready to click away, when an advert popped up on the right-hand corner of the website. It took a couple of attempts to read it, her eyes having a little trouble focussing after she'd sloshed that wine down so quickly. Once her understanding of the words in front of her dawned, however, her brain sobered up rapidly. A women-only sex club, with three rooms offering different experiences. One of which was all about BDSM.

Okay, that might work. Yes, indeed.

What the actual fuck am I doing?

Suzanne stared across the road at the black door. It was a cold night, and she tucked her hands deep into her pockets to keep them warm. *It's October. I should have realised I'd need to bring bloody gloves.*

She'd had to leave the car a couple of streets over, parking around here proving to be a nightmare. The club, the one that lurked behind that plain black door, was located in a mainly residential area, which had been a bit of a shock when she'd driven by earlier. Did the locals have any idea what was practically on their doorstep? Not that Suzanne really had a clue either. All she'd garnered from the ad was a click-through to a bare-bones website that provided an address and an overview of the club's rules.

Guilt stirred deep in her belly, but she quashed it. When Joanna had told her earlier in the week that she'd be out tonight on a working dinner with some of the people she met at the conference, Suzanne's brain had immediately offered her this option for how to spend her own time. But she had come here with a relatively clear conscience: she had absolutely no intention of doing anything in this place other than watching.

It wasn't about finding an alternative to her wife. Far from it. It was research, in fact, and nothing more.

Yes, so, given you only want to watch, why are you freezing your backside off outside at ten o'clock on a Saturday night when you could be in there where it's warm? Or possibly very hot?

She mustered all of her inbuilt confidence and strode across the street. A press of the buzzer triggered someone to slide back a small window at eye level in the middle of the door. Startling blue eyes met hers.

"Hello. Do you know where you are?" The woman's voice was lower than her own and a little husky.

"Hi, my name's Suzanne. I saw an ad for the club and was hoping to come in for the evening."

"Of course. One moment please."

The shutter closed, and a second later the door swung open.

Suzanne stepped into a dimly lit hallway and was greeted by the woman with the blue eyes. She was maybe ten years older than Suzanne, attractive, and with a welcoming smile on her full lips.

"Welcome to the club," the woman said. "I'm Mandy, the owner."

"Hi, Mandy. Nice to meet you." Suzanne glanced round. To her left, there was an office with two desks. A woman with long, dark hair sat at one of the desks, tapping the keys on a laptop.

"My assistant, Nina."

The young woman looked up and smiled at Suzanne, then returned to her work.

"So," Mandy said, "do you have any questions? Anything I need to clarify for you?"

Suzanne swallowed. "I'm only here to watch. I'm married." The words blurted out. "It's not about hooking up. I know your rules said there are no-touching zones, and I just want to make sure I don't get that part wrong."

Mandy's smile was reassuring and lacking in any kind of judgement. "Of course. Plenty of our clients want the same thing, so don't be concerned. In each room, both the stools at the bar and those around the centre table are no-touch zones. If you are sitting there, everyone will leave you alone. And if they don't, please report them to the bartender or to us here in the office."

"Okay. Great. That sounds easy enough."

Mandy lifted one shoulder. "We want everyone to have a positive experience here, and we've found over the years that the simplest rules are the best. And everyone seems to respect them, so it works."

"Good to hear." Suzanne relaxed and smiled at Mandy. "I'm a confident person, but this is well out of my comfort zone." The admission came easily; something about Mandy's persona made it so.

"And it's the same for many of the women who come here. Everyone has their own reasons, and no one will be judged for them." She clasped her hands together. "Now, it's twenty pounds for membership for the evening, and then you can buy whatever drinks you like at the bar. There's a locker room for your coat and belongings—we'd prefer no bags are taken into the rooms, and certainly no phones."

"Of course!" Suzanne shrugged off her coat, showed Mandy her phone stowed safely in her bag, and followed her to the locker room. She pulled a couple of notes from her purse and handed them over, then secured everything away, the small locker key tucking neatly into one back pocket of her jeans, some cash into the other.

"Is there any room in particular you want to visit this evening, or are you interested in a general look around?" Mandy asked as they stepped back out into the hallway.

Suzanne's face burned, but there was nothing she could do about that. "I'm actually interested in the Red Room." Her voice was a croak, and she cleared her throat.

"Okay, you'll find that easily. That door"—Mandy pointed to the one at the end of the hallway—"takes you into the first room, Green, and then you'll see a red light above a door on the far right-hand side which will take you into Red. But of course, feel free to explore the other rooms at your leisure too."

"Thanks. That's… Thank you." Suzanne managed a smile.

"Enjoy your evening." Mandy turned away and headed back to the office.

Suzanne let out a slow breath, then opened the door that led into the Green Room.

Nothing in her life, despite her overall confidence and unshakeable nature, had prepared her for walking into a room where the heady scent of sex hung so heavily in the air. She halted on the periphery of the room, near the bar, and stared. There were women having sex *everywhere*. Against every wall. In every corner. Women of all shapes, sizes, colours.

My God, if this place had existed when I was eighteen and trying to figure everything out, I might have saved myself a huge amount of time and worry.

She forced herself to move, not wanting to look like a gawping tourist, and made her way to the bar. A drink was required before she dared step into the Red Room—if she even made it that far; even the so-called vanilla room was a mind-blowing experience and almost too much for her overloaded senses. Sounds reached her now as she neared the bar, sounds of lust, and passion, and—she nearly fanned herself—orgasms galore.

Fuck me.

There was one empty stool at the bar, and she pulled it out and sat quickly.

She ordered a white wine, then watched the room for a while, gradually getting used to the idea that it was okay to do so. Everything she saw thrilled her in ways the Porn Hub stuff had never done. All these wonderful women finding what they wanted and not caring one iota about doing it this way. The empowerment in the room was more intoxicating than the sex itself.

During the time that it took Suzanne to drink half of her wine, the three women who'd occupied the other stools at the bar had all finished theirs and headed out into the room to find a playmate, leaving her watching alone.

Suzanne sucked in a breath. *Come on. You can't sit here all night.* Well, she could, obviously. But her curiosity had fought through her nerves, and now she was keen to explore. That was the whole point of the evening, and delaying it was senseless.

She caught the bartender's eye. "Can I take my drink with me to another room?"

"Absolutely! Wander as much as you like." The woman gave her a quick nod. "Enjoy your evening."

"Thank you." Suzanne swivelled off the stool, carefully picked up her glass, and directed her trembling legs towards the door with the red light above it.

The sound of something slapping against flesh was the first thing that penetrated her awareness. The second thing was how inappropriately dressed she might be in a room like this.

Low-slung jeans and a white shirt unbuttoned to her cleavage were her go-to outfit for any casual evening out, but one quick look around and she knew she'd stick out like a sore thumb. Everyone she could see wore either some kind of leather or satin ensemble or was stark naked.

Fucking. Hell.

Before her chin could hit the floor, she hurried over to the bar and yanked out a stool. She was thankfully the only one there right now. She pointed at her half-full glass when the bartender, this time a cute blonde with a smattering of freckles on her pale skin, approached. The bartender nodded, then leaned against the bar at the end and cast her gaze around the room. Watching the action? Or monitoring for safety reasons? Suzanne couldn't be sure.

She followed the bartender's gaze, and for a moment shut her eyes; it was even more overwhelming than the Green Room, much as she'd suspected.

Across the room from her, strapped to some kind of large X-shaped contraption that seemed to be made of polished wood, a woman with shoulder-length brunette hair was being…whipped? Suzanne wasn't sure what her partner held in her hands, but whatever it was, the woman on the receiving end writhed, as far as her restraints would allow, in obvious ecstasy at each lick of the implement across her bare body. Whatever it was reddened her skin but didn't split it. The woman seemed to enjoy it the most across her backside, and Suzanne squirmed in her seat each time the woman cried out at the touch.

Suzanne had no trouble imagining how delicious that sensation would be, much to her surprise, and her clit made that abundantly clear. In all her fantasising, it had been the dominance that had turned her on the most; pain, gentle or otherwise, hadn't factored in. But watching it play out before her now, her imagination graduated to another level as her pussy became wetter and wetter.

She forced her gaze away to see what else was happening around her. To her left stood a tall black woman with close-cropped grey hair wearing tight-fitting black trousers, a sleeveless top of some kind, and knee-length boots. At the woman's feet knelt another black woman in perhaps her early thirties with beautifully big breasts from which Suzanne could barely pull her gaze. The submissive woman sat back on her feet a little, her back ramrod straight, her hands laid palm upwards on her thighs. Her legs were slightly parted, and even from this distance, Suzanne could see the wetness shining on her shaved pussy. She could also see the almost blissful state of the woman as she gazed up at her mistress, awaiting whatever command she would give.

The submissive's position did something to Suzanne, something almost profound, and a strange calm settled over her as she observed the woman's posture. *God, I want to be there.* Not with the grey-haired woman, of course, but waiting at Joanna's feet like that, not knowing exactly what Joanna wanted but knowing she would do whatever it was. She would obey. She would be Joanna's plaything to use however she saw fit.

A shudder of excitement ran down her body and she had to shift in her seat once more; she was so swollen, it was almost painful.

She breathed out slowly and took another sip of her wine. Her reactions to the scenes before her had told her the main thing she'd come here to discover: the reality was as exciting as the fantasy. Or, at least, other people's reality. Her mood deflated. Yes, for other people, those who had that understanding with their partners, even if they were only partners for this one evening. She, however, did not have that. Because she'd never found the nerve to just get it out there and ask Joanna.

What had she seen on someone's website recently? Something like, you can probably have better sex if you start that awkward conversation rather than not having it at all.

Could she do it? Go home and have that talk with Joanna? Not tonight, not out of the blue. But maybe she could make sure they had some time to themselves, maybe a nice meal, a glass of wine, some romantic music—if they ever had a quiet evening to themselves again.

She puffed out a breath and picked up her wine again. She'd have to fight her own upbringing and Joanna's background and reticence and find some courage from somewhere to just do it. She downed a mouthful of her drink. But first, she'd observe as much as she could, here tonight, so she would already have a good idea of her boundaries and her needs.

She slid off the stool and strode to the centre table, which was actually offset in this room to make space for all the specialised equipment and benches available for use. As the whole table came into view for the first time, she stumbled to a stop, her heart thudding.

Joanna occupied the last stool on the right.

"As you can see," Roz said, "it's different for everyone." She pointed to a couple using one of the benches in front of them. "That Domme is giving her submissive exactly what she wants, even though for me, being called those names would do absolutely nothing for me."

Joanna nodded, her attention solely focused on the two women in question. The Domme had restrained her sub face down over a padded bench and was busy telling her what a whore and a slut she was for spreading her legs so easily. The words enflamed Joanna's feminist principles, but she had promised herself to learn what she could from this evening, and that meant learning what she didn't like as much as what she thought she might like.

She turned to Roz, once again so grateful that this woman, who she'd only met about forty-five minutes earlier, had been astute enough to realise Joanna was out of her depth but desperate to learn. In her early thirties, with long, straight brown hair and dark-brown eyes, Roz was the admin manager for an optician in everyday life. Just an ordinary person, as Joanna had been quick to realise—no one in the BDSM lifestyle was anything but.

Roz was currently without a Domme, and after one awkward moment when she assumed Joanna was here looking for a new sub, they'd quickly settled into a teacher and student relationship. Roz loved her lifestyle, that much was obvious, and she was encouraging of Joanna's attempt to address her own needs.

Somehow, opening up to the stranger hadn't been difficult—after all, Joanna had reasoned, this was a one-time visit to the club, and she'd therefore never see Roz again. Oh, of course, she'd blushed and stammered her way through her explanation of what she'd not been able to verbalise to her wife. But Roz had simply listened, then asked some questions, then listened some more, and Joanna had felt more at ease about her desires in these past forty minutes than she had in the previous twenty years.

"I suppose it's all about communication, isn't it?" Joanna asked.

"It really is. And also about letting go, whether you are the Domme or the sub. Letting go of preconceived ideas of what sexual desire is and how it's manifested in all of us. We are all individuals, and we all have every right to be turned on by whatever it is that gets us wet." She gave Joanna a quick smile. "It's then up to us to negotiate with our partners as to how much of that they are willing to satisfy, and vice versa. It should be the same in anyone's sex life, but I bet you most couples never even talk about it."

Joanna's stomach roiled with shame—she and Suzanne hadn't talked about sex in years, and she knew that was pretty much all on her. She was the restrained one, the one who still carried so many demons around about being a sexual being. Something she was working hard to change, but having been caught masturbating by her highly religious grandmother when she was twelve years old had inflicted a huge amount of damage on her sexual confidence.

As she had grown into adulthood, it had proven a hard pattern to break, but she was determined to do it now. And being here, in this incredible place, was one part of that. As would actually sitting down and having a conversation with her wife.

She was about to ask another question when someone stepped into the right side of her peripheral vision.

"What the hell is this?" an angry voice said.

Joanna's stomach dropped to the floor, and she whipped around in her seat. "Suzanne?" Her voice was an embarrassing squeak.

"Joanna?" Suzanne glared at her, hands on her hips. "What the hell are you doing here? I thought you were out with the conference people?"

"I…" Joanna swallowed, but then a lightbulb switched on in her brain and her shock gave way to anger. "Hang on, you're asking *me*? What are *you* doing here?"

Suzanne blinked and shuffled her feet. She ran her hands through her hair, which hung loose over one shoulder, just the way Joanna loved it.

Did she do that for someone else? Is she cheating on me?

Suzanne's gaze flicked to Roz and back. "Who's this?" The words were expelled on a snarl.

Joanna had never seen jealousy in Suzanne—she'd never given her a reason to experience it, after all—and it tore at her to see her wife so fearful. She had her own concerns about why Suzanne herself was here, but first, she could at least address her question. "This is Roz. I met her about forty-five minutes ago. I've been asking some questions about what happens here. That's all."

"Absolutely true," Roz said gently. "Please don't be concerned."

Suzanne's jaw clenched.

"Everything all right here?" another voice said.

All three women looked up to find the bartender standing on the other side of the table. The blonde wasn't big in stature, but her stance made obvious her confidence in her own authority in this space.

It was Roz who spoke up first. "Hi, Cassie. It's all good. Joanna and her wife have just managed to shock each other by appearing here separately, that's all."

Joanna wanted to laugh hysterically. *Yes, shocked. You could say that.*

"Okay." Cassie looked from one to the other. "Well, can you either sit down"—she directed that at Suzanne—"or find somewhere for the two of you to talk where you won't be disturbing the other clients?" Her voice was firm, but it held a hint of empathetic understanding that touched Joanna.

"We will," Joanna said quickly, seeing Suzanne's jaw clench again. "Sorry."

Cassie nodded and walked back towards her bar.

Roz jumped up. "Here, take my seat." She looked over at Suzanne.

Joanna watched her wife as emotions played out on her face. There was resentment, confusion, and…hurt. "Please, Suzanne." She gestured to the stool, trying to keep her voice calm. "We clearly need to talk."

As if thinking it might be against her better judgement, Suzanne exhaled, gave a curt nod, then took the stool Roz had vacated.

"Just talk." Roz's smile was warm and encouraging. "It's all about communication." She patted Joanna's shoulder, then walked off.

Suzanne's hands twisted together where they rested on the table, and she wouldn't meet Joanna's eye.

Joanna had never seen her so tightly wound. Talk, Roz had said. *Okay, well, here goes.* "Look at me. Please."

After a few moments, Suzanne turned her head and met her gaze. Her eyes were narrowed, her mouth set in a tight line.

Joanna tried to give an encouraging smile but wasn't sure if she succeeded in doing more than quirk up one corner of her mouth. "I realised some time ago that I wasn't completely satisfied with our sex life." Her voice croaked, and she took a quick sip of her wine. "It was lovely, but I hated how passive I always was. I hardly ever initiated things, and you were wonderfully understanding, but I always felt as if I weren't carrying my share in that part of our relationship."

Suzanne jolted in her seat. She made to say something, but Joanna held up one hand.

"Wait, let me say it, okay?"

Suzanne licked her lips, then nodded.

"I told you what happened with my grandmother. But I don't think I realised just how far it had affected me until the last year or so. I knew I'd been denying so much to myself, so much that I found sexy and exciting. I…I have fantasies—things I want to do. And I've never been able to express that to you." Her face was warm; she took another sip of wine. "I started doing some research. You know I like to process things before I talk about them."

For the first time since she'd arrived, Suzanne managed a small smile.

"So I, um, investigated a range of websites and books that could help me understand what I needed. Being here tonight was part of that research. I was going to talk to you about it all, once I'd figured out just what I wanted."

To her surprise, Suzanne burst out laughing, the sound rich and musical to Joanna's ears. "Oh my God, I can't believe this." Suzanne stared at her. "Me too."

Joanna's brain, overloaded from the shock of how the evening had unfolded, couldn't process that statement. "I'm sorry, what?"

Suzanne leaned in. "I said, my love, me too. You've just related what I've been going through the last year or so. And it's why I'm here tonight too. Research." She shook her head and her shoulders slumped. "When did we stop really talking to each other?"

Joanna took a moment to process everything Suzanne had said: she had the same feelings, had been through the same process. And they'd never mentioned a word to each other. "I suppose we let our jobs, and our everyday life, take over. We're both guilty of that. As well, I didn't know how to express what it was I wanted to change, so it seemed easier never to mention it."

"Same for me, I guess. For some reason, my usual confidence deserted me on this one." Suzanne bit her bottom lip. "I think because I… Well, I'm worried that what I want isn't something you'd want. And I'm worried that once it's out there, it will do more damage than good if you don't want the same thing. You know what I mean?"

Joanna nodded, understanding exactly. "Roz said most couples never really talk about their true desires, either from embarrassment or fear."

Suzanne's eyes took on a haunted look. "And you really did only meet her here tonight?" Her voice was small, lacking in its usual power.

Aware of the limitations of where they sat, of the club's strict rules about no-touching zones, Joanna leaned as close as she dared and stared deep into Suzanne's pale blue eyes. "Yes. I have never cheated on you. I will never cheat on you. You are my one true love, till death do us part. I love you, sweetheart. I always have and I always will."

Suzanne visibly relaxed. "I'm sorry I asked. I shouldn't have doubted you, but seeing you here just threw me. And please, believe me when I say it's exactly the same for me. Tonight was all about finding out some things about myself. I don't need or want anyone else. Ever."

Joanna's love for this strong, determined woman welled up in a way it hadn't in some time. She'd never stopped loving Suzanne, of course, but their love had become so ingrained, it was almost as unconscious as the act of breathing. *We need to express it more fully, more often.* It was very much necessary—as was her overwhelming need to hold and kiss her wife. "Come with me." She slid off her stool.

Suzanne hesitated, then moved quickly to follow her.

To their right, a few metres away, was an empty length of wall with an alcove at chest height containing certain hygiene supplies Joanna had seen other clients making use of. She waited until Suzanne joined her at the patch of wall just to the left of the alcove, then wrapped her arms around her and pulled her close.

"Oh!" Suzanne moaned as Joanna pressed their bodies tight together. "Oh God, babe, I love you so much," she whispered.

Joanna kissed her hungrily, demanding immediate entry to Suzanne's hot mouth, and her arousal, which had been simmering for the last hour or so as she'd observed the actions in the room, flared to near boiling point.

Suzanne's lips, so full and plump, felt so good crushed beneath her own. Suzanne's body, all soft curves and warmth, sank into hers, another moan escaping Suzanne's throat as Joanna pushed her back against the wall and pressed even closer.

It wasn't like Joanna to be this strong, to go for what she wanted. She hadn't even thought it through; she'd just wanted to kiss the heck out of her beautiful wife.

Suzanne returned her passion, kissing her as if they'd never kissed before, seeking, searching, taking.

Joanna arched into her, running her fingers through Suzanne's soft hair, resting her other hand on Suzanne's waist, making sure she kept their hips melded together.

When Suzanne pulled away a tad, gulping in air, her eyes were wide. "That was... Oh wow."

Tell her. Tell her now. Joanna swallowed hard. "I...I want to be the one in charge more. In bed." Her face burned, but she plunged on. "I want to tell you what to do, have you obey me and know that you have to do what I want."

Joanna's heart pounded. She'd done it. She'd said the words. Would her confident, always-take-charge wife be receptive? Or would her natural tendency to be in control, to manage every situation, mean she would be unable to submit in the way Joanna desired? Joanna had long admitted to herself that seeing Suzanne relinquish that air of control was a big part of her fantasy. She admired Suzanne, was in awe of her confidence and surety, but how delicious would it be to have her unravelled and begging at her feet?

Suzanne's grip on Joanna's waist tightened. "You do?"

"Yes." Her voice wobbled; she was unsure what Suzanne's startled reaction meant. Would she now run screaming from the room? Was this the end of their—?

"Oh God, I want that too. So badly." Suzanne flushed; her arms trembled. "To give you everything. To be everything you want. I—I want you to use me in any way you want."

"You do?" Joanna's heartbeat pounded in her ears.

Suzanne nodded, then licked her lips. "I never thought this would be something you'd like."

"I never thought you'd want to give up your control."

"I've never felt in control in the bedroom. I've always just felt we were equals. We give and take, but it's soft and gentle and easy. And I don't mean that's not lovely, because it is. But, oh wow, you taking charge, giving orders I have to obey..." She nuzzled up to Joanna's ear. "That makes me so wet just thinking about it."

A new jolt of arousal shot down to Joanna's clit, and she clenched Suzanne's hips. "Me too." She pulled back to look Suzanne in the eye. "I'm nervous, though."

"Of?"

Joanna sighed. "Of getting it wrong. Of being rubbish at it. I'm—I'm scared you'll laugh at my attempts. I don't have that power in my voice that you do or—"

Suzanne placed a finger on Joanna's lips. "I don't think it's about having a big booming voice. I think it's more about us making a contract, if you like. I agree that you are in charge, and you agree that I am your responsibility. You don't need a big voice to tell me what to do. Just tell me. I'll obey. And I swear to you, I'm not going to laugh. I want this so much, babe. I want both of us to get what we really want from it, so the last thing I want is to intentionally do anything to put you off what we're exploring."

"Okay." Joanna exhaled. "We just need to keep talking, don't we? All the way through."

"We do."

"So, um, apart from me being in charge, what exactly are you interested in?" Joanna motioned behind her to the activities that filled the room with noises and the scent of desire. "All of this?"

"Not all of it, no. But some of it, yes." Suzanne pursed her lips. "Okay, honestly speaking, the idea for me was more of the domination—being told what to do and when to do it. I don't think pain is my thing, but having said that, I saw someone being, um, whipped a little earlier—on her backside in particular—and that really turned me on more than I would have thought." She paused; her face was flushed again, but she seemed determined to just get it all out there. "Being tied up or restrained definitely appeals. Blindfolded too. And being exposed, like being forced to be on my hands and knees and knowing you're looking at me, wet and open for you. That's a huge turn-on." Suzanne stared at her. "Does any of that work for you?"

Joanna's blood seared through her veins at an almost unbearable temperature. "All of it," she whispered. Her heart raced so fast she feared for her health. "And I like the idea of, um, telling you off. Making up indiscretions that you have to be punished for." She closed her eyes for a moment. "I'd really like to take you over my knee and spank you, have you count off each smack. I read that in an erotic story and it, well, it did things to me."

Suzanne groaned and pulled Joanna back in for another kiss. "That sounds so hot when you say it."

"Yes?"

"Oh my God, yes."

Joanna smiled, her joy at how the evening had turned from a huge low point to this wonderful high filling her heart. They had talked and they were going to do this. Confidence, the like of which she'd never experienced, filled her, expanding her chest, making her feel as if she was six inches taller.

An idea formed, startling her with its urgency. But this night of surprises seemed to have no boundaries, so…

She jutted her chin up. "You were rather rude to my new friend Roz when you first arrived." She worked hard to add some firmness to her tone even though her voice was quiet and her stomach tight with nerves.

Suzanne blinked, opened her mouth as if to protest, then shut it again. To Joanna's astonishment, she then dropped her head and shoulders. "You're right. I was."

She flicked a glance up at Joanna, and in that glance, Joanna knew they were on exactly the same page and that they were about to embark on a whole new chapter in their relationship.

"Rudeness is one of those indiscretions I mentioned earlier. An indiscretion that warrants a certain degree of punishment. Wouldn't you agree?" She was so proud her voice didn't wobble—she was nervous, yes, but she'd just been given the green light to try this, and she was damned if she would pass up the opportunity.

Suzanne's cheeks flushed, but Joanna knew it wasn't from embarrassment. She would bet their house Suzanne's underwear was extremely wet right now.

"Yes…?" Suzanne looked at her expectantly.

Joanna had thought long and hard about this. About what persona she would take. Being just Joanna wouldn't work for her. She needed an alter ego to boost her confidence. "You will call me Mistress." She knew it wasn't original, but that was irrelevant; it was what had worked for her in all her fantasies, so she would stick with it.

A shudder ran through Suzanne. She let out a whimper and licked her lips. "Yes, Mistress."

It did something to her, being called that for the first time. Lit up something inside her, something that flared out and ran across her skin and through her veins. It felt right, as if that was how she was supposed to have been addressed all along. She took a deep breath to quell the emotion that threatened to break out in the form of tears. *Come on, let's do this properly.*

She glanced from left to right. Oh, yes, there. Perfect. She stepped back, instantly missing Suzanne's warmth but knowing it would soon be replaced by something guaranteed to raise her temperature even further. She grabbed the pack of antibacterial wipes from the alcove next to them and handed them to Suzanne. "That bench there." She pointed to her left, Suzanne's right. "Clean it with these." She swallowed. "On your knees. But first, take off your jeans. Leave your heels on."

The thought of Suzanne's almost-naked backside swinging from left to right as she worked to clean the bench made Joanna ache with need.

Suzanne's eyebrows shot up. She looked at the bench, then quickly around the room.

"You can say no if you're not comfortable. We need to know each other's boundaries." Joanna brushed a fingertip down Suzanne's cheek.

"I know." Suzanne cast one more glance at the room, then held out her hand for the pack of wipes. "Yes, Mistress." Her voice was soft, demure, completely lacking in any of the boldness it normally contained. The transformation was extraordinary, and with her easy acquiescence to Joanna's demand, definitely one of the hottest moments they'd shared.

Joanna swallowed. "Good. But before you get started, we should agree on a safe word."

"Wow, you really did research this, didn't you?"

"Of course." Joanna grinned. "You married a geek, remember?"

Laughing, Suzanne leaned in and kissed her. "I did. And I love my geek." She straightened and thought for a moment. "Broccoli."

"All right." Joanna had no idea of the word's significance, but that was irrelevant. It was their safe word. Locked in. And now they could really start. She pointed at the jeans. "Off."

"Yes, Mistress." Suzanne dropped the pack of wipes onto the bench, then turned to face her.

Joanna watched, her mouth dry, as Suzanne slowly eased her jeans open and then off her hips. She held Joanna's gaze as she dropped the jeans to the floor and carefully kicked them off over her shoes. The latter were one of Joanna's favourites—dark purple suede with a thin strap over the ankle and a two-and-a-half-inch heel. *Oh, yes, she definitely needs to be half-naked in heels a lot more often.*

Suzanne turned away and bent to pick up the wipes.

Joanna sucked in a breath. The view was magnificent: two perfectly round cheeks framed by the hem of the shirt at the top. The thong Suzanne wore was a dark colour, but that was all Joanna could tell in the dim light. Besides, she wouldn't be wearing it soon, so who cared what colour it was?

Suzanne looked back over her shoulder. "Is this to your liking, Mistress?"

"Very much." Joanna's voice was a raw croak.

There was a smirk on Suzanne's lips as she dropped to her knees.

Joanna chalked up one more smack to the list for that cheekiness, then enjoyed the show as her wife moved around the bench.

With her back to Joanna, she presented that glorious view of her backside. When she moved around the bench to clean it from the other side, her position afforded Joanna a direct line of sight down her shirt to her cleavage. Suzanne's breasts, big and soft, had always thrilled Joanna, but no more so than in this precise moment.

She licked her lips.

Suzanne scrunched up the final wipe and added it to the waste pile she'd created against the wall. Then she sat back on her heels and looked up at Joanna from across the bench. "Finished, Mistress."

Joanna's pussy clenched. Suzanne, on her knees, gazing up at her, awaiting her next instruction, was probably the sexiest thing she'd ever experienced. *And it's only going to get sexier.*

With confidence surging through her, she walked the two paces to the bench and sat facing Suzanne. She shifted a couple of times to make sure she was comfortable—and to ensure there would be room to have her wife splayed across her lap. "Come here."

Suzanne shuffled forward on her knees. Inside her shirt, her breasts, encased in one of her lacy white bras, swayed with the movement.

Joanna's clit throbbed at the sight. "Over my lap."

Suzanne moaned and clambered up and over Joanna's thighs. It couldn't be done gracefully, but it still turned Joanna on to watch her wife crawl into position. Suzanne laid her head on her folded arms, then looked back at her. "Is this okay, Mistress?" Her eyes had darkened, and her cheeks and neck were flushed, a sure sign she was aroused.

Joanna swept Suzanne's hair away from her face, letting it fall in a sexy tumble over one shoulder, then looked down at her body, laid so beautifully across her lap.

Suzanne's backside was pushed up, her thighs parted, and she'd bent her knees a little, presumably to balance herself. It brought the heels up, and Joanna added that to her growing list of favourite-ways-to-see-my-wife.

"Very good." Joanna's hand trembled as she lifted Suzanne's shirt higher, uncovering all her backside.

Suzanne groaned, and her scent reached Joanna's nostrils. Her wife must be very wet indeed.

"Oh, you like this too, do you?" Joanna asked before running a fingertip up Suzanne's leg from the back of her knee to the gorgeous crease where one buttock met a thigh.

"Oh God, yes, Mistress." Suzanne's voice had taken on a deep, husky timbre, and she arched into Joanna's touch.

More wetness pooled between Joanna's thighs. She was tempted simply to keep stroking Suzanne, to run her fingers over the soft skin of her thighs and backside, then perhaps dip into the wetness of her pussy. But that wasn't what this was supposed to be about. She'd fantasised about this so many times, and now Suzanne was spread out before her, at her mercy.

"You're not supposed to enjoy punishment." Joanna braced herself and lifted her right hand. "Are you?"

"No, Mistr—"

Smack.

"Ah! Oh God!" Suzanne bucked on Joanna's lap.

Joanna couldn't believe she'd done it. She stared down at the red mark on Suzanne's left buttock. *Oh my God, I just spanked my wife.* Her hand stung a little but in a good way. Her breathing was ragged, and her pussy was so wet she knew her underwear was soaked all the way through to her trousers.

She looked at Suzanne, gauging her reaction. Was her cry one of pleasure or discomfort? Did she want to stop?

Suzanne opened her eyes and locked gazes with Joanna. "One. Thank you, Mistress."

Joanna thought she might orgasm there and then. Instead, she threw Suzanne a wicked smile and raised her hand once more.

Smack.

A matching red mark on Suzanne's right buttock. Another ecstatic cry from her lips.

Suzanne's body quivered. "Two! Thank you, Mistress."

The thank yous were a lovely touch. Perhaps it was something Suzanne had read about somewhere, and Joanna was glad she had. Each word of gratitude set off jolts of arousal that tightened Joanna's pussy.

Smack. Smack.

Lighter slaps this time; an article Joanna had read mentioned alternating the power, for multiple reasons, all of which had sounded sensible to Joanna.

"Three, four! Thank you, Mistress." Suzanne's pussy was so wet, Joanna could see it now shining in the dim light of the room, and the scent was intoxicating.

"This is turning you on, isn't it? Being punished? Look at you, lying all exposed on my lap, your pussy wet, your backside red." The words came easily. Some she'd read, some seemed to just come from somewhere deep inside, untapped until now.

"Oh God, Mistress. *Please!*" Suzanne sounded desperate, almost tortured, but Joanna knew that wasn't a bad thing.

"Please what?"

"Please touch me. Oh God, I want to come!"

"Two more, sweetheart." Joanna smoothed her hand over one of Suzanne's buttocks. "You can take two more, can't you?" She'd already decided six would do. Any more and she'd worry about hurting Suzanne; they could talk about limits later.

"Yes! Yes, anything you want." Suzanne locked her gaze on Joanna's once more. "I love you. I'll do anything for you, Mistress." She almost sobbed with need.

Joanna's heart clenched, and she fought the urge to sweep Suzanne into her arms and kiss her senseless. Later. When they were home. Something told her they were in for a long, delicious night of discovery, and that kind of intimacy could wait until then. For now, she wanted—no, *needed*—to complete this first step, to give them both this introduction to kinky pleasure they'd secretly desired all this time.

She grasped Suzanne's shoulder with her left hand, then raised her right. She brought it down swiftly and landed a perfect slap against the fleshiest part of Suzanne's left buttock once more.

"Ohhh!" Suzanne's head arched back. "Five!"

Joanna was already on her downswing before Suzanne had managed to force out that last word.

Smack!

"Ahh!" Suzanne slumped forward. "Six. Thank you, Mistress."

Joanna didn't hesitate. She yanked down Suzanne's lacy thong, shimmying it down her thighs to her knees as Suzanne moaned and writhed on her lap.

With one finger, Joanna trailed a path back up the back of Suzanne's thigh but didn't stop when she reached her buttock. She swept into the copious wetness that awaited her between Suzanne's thighs and held tight to her when she bucked into the touch.

"Oh, fuck! Yes! Mistress, please!"

Another time, she would make Suzanne wait. She would tease and play and make her beg. But not tonight. No, tonight they both needed this—and soon. "Open your legs. As far as you can."

Suzanne groaned and did as she was told; the thong's fabric around her knees stretched to its near breaking point.

Joanna took a moment to admire Suzanne's wet pussy awaiting her attention, then ran two fingers in between her swollen pussy lips. The heat that greeted her made her salivate. She slipped one finger inside; Suzanne was so open, Joanna's finger barely touched the sides of her inner walls, and so she quickly added a second, then a third.

"Oh baby, yes!"

Joanna would forgive her for forgetting her title. For now.

Slowly, she fucked Suzanne. After all these years together, she knew what her wife liked—slow thrusts until she tightened too much to take that many fingers, then to keeping one inside while working her clit with the others.

It was all familiar, but this time, it all felt brand new. Tonight, they'd given each other something they'd never imagined, and it truly felt as if they were on a different level of understanding and connection.

As she pushed in and out of Suzanne, her fingers so wetly enveloped, her own hips began their own slow grinding, her clit pressing against Suzanne's body. It wasn't quite enough pressure, but actually, the anticipation was tortuously sublime.

Suzanne grunted and moaned beneath her with each deep thrust inside her, repeating "yes, baby," and "oh God, more, please," over and over.

Intense heat built between them, as did a pleasure that flowed like liquid honey all over Joanna's body. Suzanne tightened around Joanna's fingers, and as Joanna pulled back to plunge deeper, she kept two fingers back, knowing it was nearly time for her wife to come.

Then she frowned. The angle was wrong from this position; she'd never get the right pressure on Suzanne's clit. But as much as she'd love to be the one to get Suzanne off, this was all about Suzanne's pleasure, not hers or her pride.

"Lift your hips a little, sweetheart," she said. "Touch yourself. I want to hear you come."

"Oh yes. Oh baby!"

Unable to resist, Joanna pulled out of Suzanne and gave her one more swift slap on her right buttock.

"Ah! Mistress! Sorry. Mistress, thank you. For letting me touch myself." Suzanne slipped her right hand under her body; Joanna could feel Suzanne's fingers bumping against her knuckles as they each worked a different part of her pussy. "I want to come for you so badly, Mistress."

"Then do it. Let me feel you." Joanna fucked her faster, enthralled by Suzanne humping against her legs, her hand working feverishly as she rubbed at her clit.

Joanna held her breath as Suzanne suddenly arched, her head thrown back.

A huge cry escaped Suzanne's lips as her orgasm slammed into her.

"Oh God," Joanna whispered as Suzanne shuddered against her. "God, you're so beautiful. I love you so much."

"I…love…you…too," Suzanne panted out. "Mistress."

Joanna smiled, then carefully pulled out from Suzanne.

Suzanne flopped down onto the bench once more, completely spread-eagle over Joanna's lap. It was an incredible sight, not one Joanna would forget in a hurry.

She stroked Suzanne's backside, gently massaging where she'd spanked. "I'm sorry this is the best I can do for aftercare right now. Obviously, I didn't expect things to turn out like this tonight."

Suzanne chuckled and turned slightly to look at her. "Me neither." She licked her lips. "That was…unbelievable." The emotion in her whisper made Joanna's throat tighten.

"It was. Thank you."

Suzanne quirked an eyebrow. "For?"

"For trusting me. For honouring me with your submission."

"Oh, my love. Thank *you*. For being so wonderful and giving me a dream-come-true experience." Suzanne pointed in the vicinity of her thong. "Could you pull that up for me, please?"

Joanna did so, and Suzanne took over once it was near enough to pull back into its proper place. "Hm, it's a little wet," Suzanne said. "I can't think why."

They laughed.

Then Suzanne wriggled until she could straddle Joanna's lap and wrap her arms around her. "You're a fantastic mistress."

"I'm glad you think so." Joanna wasn't usually one to feel prideful, but even she thought she'd done a pretty convincing job. Suzanne's confirmation was the icing on the cake.

"Oh my God, yes! You were incredible! I had to keep looking at you to make sure it was still you. The transformation was amazing. I loved it." She leaned down and kissed Joanna, her lips moving slowly, tenderly.

Joanna held her tight and returned the kiss, stroking Suzanne's tongue with her own, her heart near to bursting with joy and love.

"So, how are you doing?" Suzanne asked when they parted. "Do you want to come? Want me to touch you?"

Joanna swallowed. "I do. But I already have plans for that."

"Oh?" Suzanne gave her a smirk.

"Yes. But for when we're home." She threw Suzanne her wickedest smile. "I want you on your knees again."

Suzanne's eyes glazed. "Oh yeah…"

"But," Joanna held up a finger, "this time in our bedroom, where we don't have to worry about what's been on that floor." She pointed downwards.

Suzanne threw back her head and laughed. "Oh God, you're adorable."

Joanna huffed. "Adorable? Let's see if you still feel the same way when I have you tied up and begging me to touch you."

Suzanne visibly swallowed. "Ready to go home now?"

Now it was Joanna's turn to laugh out loud. "Yes, I am. Get your clothes on and let's get out of here."

"Yes, Mistress."

EPILOGUE

MANDY

One year later

"Right, I'm off." Nina picked up her handbag and car keys.

"Thanks again for doing the full shift." Mandy stood and walked her to the door. "And thank Cassie for me for not kicking up a fuss."

Nina rolled her eyes. "As if she would. You know we both love this place, and you, and will always help you out whenever you need it."

"I know, but given that she's only three weeks away from bringing your gorgeous child into this world, I would definitely have understood if you wanted to get home much earlier."

"Fair enough." Nina took hold of the door handle, then turned back. "Hey, isn't it tomorrow you're having a FaceTime call with Dee?"

"It is, yes."

"Then say hi from both of us, please. And tell her we still can't believe she put working on a lesbian cruise ship above coming back to this place. Seriously, I may never forgive her." Nina grinned.

Mandy laughed. "Oh, yes, as if you wouldn't have jumped at exactly the same chance if you'd been single. Wall-to-wall lesbians, sun, beaches, a different port every day?"

Nina tapped her chin. "Hm, you may have a point." She smirked. "Don't tell Cassie I said that."

"Your secret is safe with me. Besides, you did all right out of it. And you've been a brilliant replacement for her."

"Aw, thanks!"

Mandy wrapped Nina in a quick hug that seemed to surprise them both. "And I know how much you love Cassie, and the life you have, so I know there isn't anywhere else you'd rather be."

Nina's eyes glistened. "True." She waved a hand in front of her face. "Don't make me cry!"

Mandy smiled, then held open the front door for her. "Go on, get on home to your woman. Give her my love. Tell her the Red Room misses its favourite bartender."

"I will. See you next week."

"Only if Cassie is okay with it." Mandy threw Nina a stern look.

Nina saluted. "Yes, ma'am!"

Mandy shut the door behind her, a smile on her lips. *God help that child with that ball of energy as its mother.* She didn't mean it, though; she could tell Nina and Cassie were going to be fantastic parents.

"Right," she said to the empty building. "Now it's my turn to get home."

She finished off checking that all the rooms were secure for the night—lights off, rubbish cleared, bars locked down, and cashboxes empty. Then she bagged up the evening's takings and shoved the heavy-duty money bag into her shoulder bag. She'd count it all up tomorrow and drop it in the night safe sometime during the day.

It was a cold night; November had started bitter and hadn't let go. Frost covered the car, and she cursed as she fumbled with the scraper to get the worst of it off for a couple of minutes until she gratefully climbed onto the heated driver's seat and pulled out.

As usual, the drive home was quiet this early on a Sunday morning. The extended opening hours she'd introduced a couple of months before due to popular demand had proved worthwhile, even though she came home even more tired than before. She really did need to start thinking about stepping back. Maybe hire another Nina, and between them they could rotate which nights they all covered. She'd maybe talk about that with Nina next week.

The hallway of her home was illuminated when she pulled onto the driveway. She smiled, warmth flooding her chest. It still got to her, that little beacon in the darkness at the end of her long night. She hurried out of the car and unlocked the front door.

Claws scrabbling on hardwood floors greeted her, and she only had a moment to brace herself before the boys came bounding around the corner.

"Hello, my beauties," Mandy whispered as they rubbed up against her, their tails wagging, tongues lolling. She rubbed their heads, ears, and flanks, dodging slobbery kisses and trying to keep the noise down.

Jed, the dark-brown Labrador, gazed up at her with adoration.

Holmes, playing true to his Boxer nature, gambolled around her, his energy palpable even at this late hour.

"Come on, boys, back to bed. We'll play in the morning, okay?" She led them back to the utility room and waited until they'd circled and settled into their beds before she left them. After a quick check to make sure they had plenty of water, she made her way upstairs.

"If I had a tail, I'd be wagging it too," Laura called as Mandy neared their bedroom.

Mandy laughed. "Oh, would you, now?"

The bedside lamp switched on, and there she was.

My love.

As usual, at a little before four on a Sunday morning, Laura looked dishevelled. But still gorgeous. Her pyjamas were rumpled; her hair stuck out in a multitude of directions. "How was the evening?"

"Good. Bumper night, actually. One hundred and twenty through the door."

Laura's eyes bugged wide. "Jesus, that's fantastic!"

"I know!" Mandy grinned, then flopped onto the bed beside her. "And, oh boy, do my feet and bones know it."

Laura pulled her closer and dropped a gentle kiss on her lips. "I'm not surprised. Want a massage?"

"No, my love. It's late. I've already woken you up and—"

"I've been asleep since ten, so that six hours feels great, don't you worry." Laura shuffled out from under the duvet. "Come on, just a little aftercare so you can feel even more rested in the morning."

Mandy gave in. "Take me, I'm yours."

Laura wagged one finger. "Massage first."

She retrieved some lotion from the en suite, then helped Mandy remove her clothes. The bedroom was warm, as usual, so Mandy didn't worry about grabbing for her pyjamas just yet.

Laura's careful attention to her needs, and her obvious admiration of Mandy's naked form, made Mandy weak with emotion. Discovering love with this woman, so relatively late in their lives, still felt like a miracle. Yes, Nina and some others had snorted knowingly when she and Laura had moved in together after only eight months of being a couple, but why wait? They fit—better than they could ever have imagined—and neither of them wanted to waste another minute apart.

"Are you okay?" Laura stilled her hands from where they worked circles on the soles of Mandy's feet.

"Yes. Why?"

"Because you look like you're about to cry."

Good grief. Mandy dashed at her damp eyes and chuckled. "I'm feeling sappy. Ignore me."

"Oh, I could never ignore you, my love." Laura planted a soft kiss on Mandy's knee.

Mandy shivered; just that simple touch, from that mouth, sparked her desire, hot and quick, pushing her emotions to one side—or, more accurately, joining with her emotions to leave her in desperate need of everything this woman could give her. "You said you weren't tired, is that right?"

Laura gazed up at her from the foot of the bed, her eyes knowing. "Correct."

Mandy nodded and crooked a finger. "Then why don't you lose the pjs and come here?"

The grin Laura gave her was decidedly naughty. She shucked off her pyjamas and stood before Mandy, her naked skin glowing in the soft lamp light.

Her body, stocky yet still firm, did things to Mandy she'd never thought she'd experience again. Not at this age. Every day, she thanked whoever, gods or goddesses, had put Laura on that train from Brighton eighteen months ago to explore a women-only sex club she'd heard about somewhere. And although she might not say it out loud that often, she also mentally thanked Laura every day for being bold that night and asking Mandy out for lunch.

When Laura laid her hot, soft skin on top of Mandy's, she couldn't help the groan that escaped from deep in her chest. Nor could she have stopped her hands from exploring her lover's body if her life depended on it. She needed this. Needed her.

Laura gazed down at her and slowly moved her hips into Mandy, the action always a precursor to something even more exciting and fulfilling. She kissed Mandy deeply and forcefully, just the way Mandy loved it.

Mandy squirmed beneath her, her body already on fire, her need exponentially growing.

"I want you." Laura's voice was husky in Mandy's ear. "I want to be inside you." She caressed one hand over Mandy's breast, then pinched her nipple between her fingertips. "I want to spread your legs wide and fuck you until you scream my name."

It was always like this: hot, intense, exquisite.

And it was exactly what Mandy wanted. Had always wanted. They'd had a fire for each other the first time they met nearly thirty years before. Now they were older, had been through some stuff, but that fire had been oh-so-easy to rekindle. It had taken the club to bring them back together, but what they'd found after that evening had been all their own doing.

Mandy smiled up at Laura, her heart thudding, her clit throbbing. "I'm yours. Take me."

Laura did.

OTHER BOOKS FROM YLVA PUBLISHING

www.ylva-publishing.com

THE CLUB

A.L. Brooks

ISBN: 978-3-95533-654-7
Length: 248 pages (72,000 words)

Welcome to The Club—leave your inhibitions and your everyday cares at the door, and indulge yourself in an evening of anonymous, no-strings, woman-on-woman action. For many visitors to The Club, this is exactly what they are looking for, and what they get. For others, however, the emotions run high, and one night of sex changes their lives in ways they couldn't have imagined.

HEART'S SURRENDER

Emma Weimann

ISBN: 978-3-95533-183-2
Length: 305 pages (63,000 words)

Neither Samantha Freedman nor Gillian Jennings are looking for a relationship when they begin a no-strings-attached affair. But soon simple attraction turns into something more. What happens when the worlds of a handywoman and a pampered housewife collide? Can nights of hot, erotic fun lead to love, or will these two very different women go their separate ways?

A no-strings-attached affair between a handywoman and a pampered housewife grows into something more in this award-winning lesbian erotica novel.

NIGHTS OF SILK AND SAPPHIRE

Amber Jacobs

ISBN: 978-3-95533-511-3
Length: 309 pages (11,300 words)

Dae is rescued from desert slavers by the mysterious Zafirah Al'Intisar and placed as a prize in the Scion's harem. At first, Dae struggles with desires she has never before experienced, but as love and lust collide these two women slowly forge a bond.

LAID BARE

Astrid Ohletz and Jae (Ed.)

ISBN: 978-3-96324-214-4
Length: 154 pages (61,000 words)

If you enjoy erotic stories about women loving women, get your hands on this collection of sensual short stories from nine of the most prominent names in lesbian fiction, many of them award-winning authors.

Stories by Jae, Lee Winter, Harper Bliss, KD Williamson, A.L. Brooks, Lola Keeley, Alison Grey, Jess Lea, and Emma Weimann

ABOUT A.L. BROOKS

A.L. Brooks was born in the UK but currently resides in Frankfurt, Germany, and over the years she has lived in places as far afield as Aberdeen and Australia. She works 9–5 in corporate financial systems and her dream is to take early retirement. Like, tomorrow, please. She loves her gym membership, and is very grateful for it as she also loves dark chocolate. She enjoys drinking good wine and craft beer, trying out new recipes to cook, and learning German. Travelling around the world and reading lots and lots (and lots) of books are also things that fight for time with her writing. Yep, she really needs that early retirement.

CONNECT WITH A.L. BROOKS

Website: www.albrookswriter.com

The Club Revisited

ISBN: 978-3-96324-562-6

Available in e-book and paperback formats.

Published by Ylva Publishing, legal entity of Ylva Verlag, e.Kfr.

Ylva Verlag, e.Kfr.
Owner: Astrid Ohletz
Am Kirschgarten 2
65830 Kriftel
Germany
www.ylva-publishing.com

First edition: 2021

Credits
Edited by Michelle Aguilar and Sheena Billet
Cover Design and Print Layout by Streetlight Graphics

Made in the USA
Monee, IL
13 October 2022